The Adventures of

Lewis and Clark

The Adventures of
Lewis and Clark

JOHN BAKELESS

Illustrated by B. Holmes

DOVER PUBLICATIONS, INC.
Mineola, New York

Published in the United Kingdom by David & Charles, Brunel House, Forde Close, Newton Abbot, Devon TQ12 4PU.

Bibliographical Note

This Dover edition, first published in 2002, is an unabridged reprint of the edition originally published by Houghton Mifflin Company, Boston/The Riverside Press, Cambridge, Mass., in 1962.

Library of Congress Cataloging-in-Publication Data

Bakeless, John Edwin, 1894–
    The adventures of Lewis and Clark / John Bakeless ; illustrations by Bea Holmes.
        p. cm.
    Originally published: Boston : Houghton Mifflin, 1962.
    Includes bibliographical references and index.
    ISBN 0-486-42159-7
    1. Lewis and Clark Expedition (1804–1806) 2. West (U.S.)—Discovery and exploration. 3. West (U.S.)—Description and travel. 4. Lewis, Meriwether, 1774–1809. 5. Clark, William, 1770–1838. I. Title.

F592.7 .B28 2002
917.804'2—dc21

                                                            2001053805

Manufactured in the United States of America
Dover Publications, Inc., 31 East 2nd Street, Mineola, N.Y. 11501

CONTENTS

Thomas Jefferson had an insatiable curiosity. He wanted to know what lay in the remote, unexplored regions west of the Mississippi. Four times he planned expeditions across the North-American continent — and only in his final attempt was he rewarded.

It was much easier the fourth time, principally because Jefferson was now the President of the United States. Shortly he could proclaim that neither the Spanish nor the French controlled the mouth of the Mississippi, or the vast Louisiana Territory, which had just been purchased from Napoleon for fifteen million dollars — the best real estate bargain our nation ever made.

Two young men, originally from his own state of Virginia, were to lead this expedition, which began in 1803 and ended successfully in 1806. They had orders to explain to the Indians that their new "White Father" lived in Washington (not in Paris or Madrid); that peace among all the Indian tribes was greatly desired, and that no harm would come to Indian nations co-operating as allies of the United States. The Indians were somewhat confused and bewildered by these incomprehensible international developments, but they became much more amiable when they were given "Indian Commissions," medals and other gifts.

In addition to their role as frontier diplomats, these two young men were to report at length on the Missouri River country, the completely unknown mountain regions, and the westward-flowing Columbia. They were also asked to keep journals, assemble Indian vocabularies from a dozen or more tribes, make botanical and zoological collections, report on the flora and fauna, and demonstrate to the world that this wilderness could be traversed.

As proved by their fascinating but ungrammatical journals, neither Lewis nor Clark was an accomplished writer. But they carried out their difficult orders so faithfully that they shed light on our whole trans-Mississippi domain, and greatly contributed to the settling of an area far larger than the original thirteen colonies.

John Bakeless, who is an ardent and dependable researcher, covered every inch of this route on a Guggenheim Fellowship. He also read the journals of Lewis, Clark, and other members of the party, besides unearthing dozens of previously unknown documents on the expedition — from a storeroom in Oregon, an attic in Virginia, a cabin in Idaho, and from various archives and libraries throughout the country. He gives a lively, accurate account of the whole significant adventure.

STERLING NORTH
General Editor

The Adventures of

Lewis and Clark

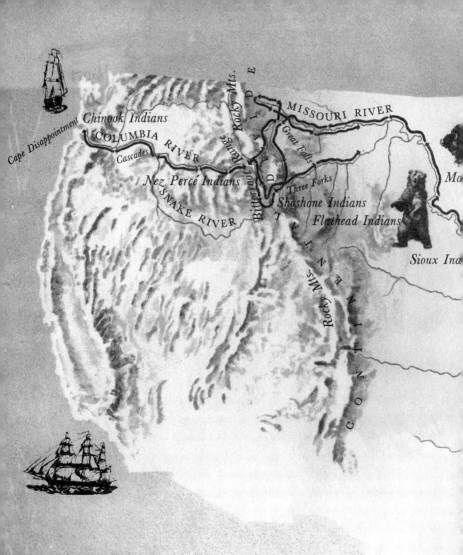

Cape Disappointment

Chinook Indians

COLUMBIA RIVER

Cascades

Nez Percé Indians

SNAKE RIVER

Rocky Mts.

Bitterroot Range

DIVIDE

Great Falls

MISSOURI RIVER

Three Forks

Shoshone Indians

Flathead Indians

CONTINENTAL

Rocky Mts.

Sioux Ind

Mo

Lewis and Cl

dians

Indians

Cheyenne Indians

SOURI RIVER

MISSOURI RIVER

Osage Indians

MISSISSIPPI RIVER

St. Louis

A

Map of

LEWIS AND CLARK'S TRACK,

Across the Western Portion of

North America

From the

MISSISSIPPI TO THE PACIFIC OCEAN;

By Order of the Executive

of the

UNITED STATES

in 1804.5.&6.

k Expedition

The Great Idea

1

W<small>HEN</small> T<small>HOMAS</small> J<small>EFFERSON</small>, the third President of the United States, entered the new White House in Washington, D.C., he was exultantly aware that now — at last! — he would be able to carry out the great idea that had been haunting him for more than twenty years.

Between the broad Mississippi and the Pacific Coast lay — what? Wonder concerning the new lands, strange tribes and stranger animals, huge mountains, and enormous wealth that must be lying there, unknown, had obsessed him for most of his life.

Three times Jefferson had tried to send explorers into the unknown American West. Three times he had failed: once, because the Revolutionary frontier hero General George Rogers Clark could not lead the expedition; again, because the Russian Empress, Catherine the Great, expelled from Siberia Mr. Jefferson's daring Yankee explorer who had planned to travel eastward across the Pacific and then all alone across North America; and last of all, because the French scientist he had engaged turned out to be Napoleon's secret agent.

When Mr. Jefferson had made this third attempt, in 1792, a neighbor's son came in to ask if *he* could go along. Mr. Jefferson knew the boy, whose family were among his friends, but he turned the applicant down because he was too young. His name was Meriwether Lewis.

That expedition, like all the others, had never even started. Now nearly a decade had passed. And President Thomas Jefferson knew he had the power to send an exploring party across the continent. It would go up the wide Missouri River, over the plains, to the foothills of the Rockies. It would cross the Rocky Mountains (no one knew just how), find the upper waters of the Columbia River (no one knew just where), construct new canoes, and then float down the Columbia to the Pacific Ocean.

Not even the Indians knew much about most of this country. For many hundreds of miles there was no Indian village, not even a temporary hunting camp. You could, at times, travel for months along the Missouri River, without seeing a human being, red or white. Here and there a few adventurous white men — traders, trappers, hunters, or explorers — had seen a little of these wild lands. Not all of them had returned to tell their story. Some were French or British, coming overland from Canada. Some were French or Spanish, venturing up the Mississippi, then a little way up the Missouri. A few Spaniards had come northward from Mexico.

The thought of this vast, unknown land had tormented Thomas Jefferson for years. He longed to know what secrets the other half of North America might hold. Everyone knew there must be immense wealth in this new country. There were stories of great mountains of salt (a precious commodity in those days). There was no doubt the country abounded in beaver, mink, martin, otter. All were valuable — beaver skins most of all. There were immense profits to be made in trade with the Indians, who would pay almost any price (in skins and furs) for white man's goods — rifles, gunpowder, steel knives and hatchets, steel arrow points, cloth, beads, tobacco. British merchants, operating from Canada, had long been growing rich in this way. Before the British, and the American colonists, drove them out, the French had been growing rich too. So prosperous was this trade that after America finally acquired possession of the country, one American fur-trading family was soon making half a million dollars a year.

The queer thing is, no one had even guessed that this new western country was full of gold, as well as furs. The first Spanish explorers had come to North America mainly to find treasure. They found it, too, in Mexico; but after searching through the southeastern areas for gold, they soon gave up exploring the Great West for this precious metal. Strange to say, although the Spaniards had owned all the enormously rich gold country of California, Montana, and the Dakotas for centuries, they never discovered any of the immense deposits there. Then came the Americans, who in less than fifty years found the great treasure.

Jefferson's first difficulty in sending an expedition to explore this area was that for many years no part of it had belonged to the United States. From the Mississippi to the Rockies it was Spanish territory; and, beyond the Rockies, the southern part of the Pacific Coast, including California, was also Spanish.

What would the King of Spain's officials do if an American expedition entered Spanish territory and began to explore it?

Thomas Jefferson had a talk with the Spanish minister in Washington, the Marqués de Casa Yrujo. This was in November, 1802, the year after Jefferson had become President. He asked the minister frankly whether it would be permissible to send an American expedition to "explore the course of the Missouri River." If he made such a move, would Spain "take it badly"? The sole aim in sending out the expedition, Mr. Jefferson explained, would be "the advancement of geography."

The Spanish minister objected strongly. The Spanish government would deeply resent any such intrusion into its territory, he told the President. As a matter of fact, the Spaniards themselves had been trying to reach the Pacific Ocean by the same route President Jefferson had in mind. The minister quickly warned his superiors in Madrid, "that the Americans may some day extend their population and their influence up to the coasts of the South Sea," as the Pacific was then called. The marqués was right. Within less

than fifty years all of the present Pacific Coast had slipped from Spanish hands and was American.

But in spite of the Spanish attitude, President Jefferson was determined to launch that expedition. A few weeks after his talk with the minister, he sent Congress a secret message, asking for an appropriation of $2500 for "extending the external commerce of the United States." This was a good safe title for the bill President Jefferson wanted Congress to pass, since it would attract no special public attention; but it was also a fairly accurate description of the President's purpose.

By bringing the Indian furs and peltry down the Missouri (out of Canadian and into American

hands), the exploration really would immensely extend "the external commerce of the United States," just as President Jefferson had hoped. When gold was later discovered the expansion was swifter. When, much later, modern farming and manufacturing spread west of the Mississippi, the expansion of American commerce was enormous.

But to return to the Jefferson era. In the midst of his plans, some very disturbing news reached the President. The Spaniards had ceded all of Louisiana to France. The immediate threat to our young and still weak American republic was obvious. Spain had been a lax and inactive neighbor, troublesome at times, but never a danger to the United States. France was a real menace. Ruled by the Emperor Napoleon, she already dominated Europe. If Napoleon ever gained a foothold in the New World he would try to dominate this hemisphere too. Then the United States would face the greatest military power in the world along the whole western border, from New Orleans to Canada.

Once established over here, Napoleon might try

to reconquer Canada. To accomplish this he would have to make war on the British. Then, if Napoleon won, the United States would find herself boxed in with the powerful French empire on our western border, and on our northern border, too. If Napoleon lost, the situation would be almost as bad. The powerful British empire would hold these same northern and western borders. Either way, American expansion westward would be blocked for ever. The predicament, as President Jefferson wrote James Monroe, was "very ominous to us."

Then Jefferson took the bold step that made possible the United States — as we know it. He instructed Robert R. Livingston, the American minister in Paris, to see if Napoleon's government would sell to us the city of New Orleans and some of the land around it. The scheme was so important that early in 1803 he rushed a Virginia friend and neighbor, James Monroe, to Paris as a special envoy.

Suddenly Napoleon made up his mind that since war with Great Britain was now sure to

Louisiana Purchase

showing the states formed out of it, and later admitted to the Union

come he would inevitably lose all Louisiana to the British navy unless he sold it. His negotiator made an offer that astonished the American negotiators: not just the territory around New Orleans, for which they were bargaining, but all of Louisiana, from the Mississippi to the Rockies for $15,000,000.

Livingston and Monroe were thunderstruck. They had no authority to pay $15,000,000. President Jefferson had authorized them to pay only $2,000,000 for New Orleans. It would take weeks for a sailing vessel to carry a letter to the President, asking for authority to pay this enormous sum. It would take weeks more for an answer to come back. By that time the chance might be lost. Napoleon might change his mind.

Boldly they seized the tremendous opportunity for their country's good and pledged the payment of $15,000,000 for a vast stretch of wild land — roughly half of the present United States — most of which no white man had ever seen. President Jefferson was delighted and fortunately Congress, too, approved.

The treaty was ratified at last on October 19, 1803. By that time Jefferson had already prepared his expedition; and its young leaders would be ready to start in only a few more months.

Mr. Jefferson had once refused to let Meriwether Lewis join a western expedition, because he was too young. Nearly ten years had passed, and the President's thoughts turned back to that tall, blond, blue-eyed young man from Albemarle. The two families had always been friends. Mrs. Lewis used to supply Mr. Jefferson with the smoked hams for which she was famous. The President knew young Meriwether was an outdoor type, strong, hardy, fond of hunting, fishing, and rambling in the woods. He remembered that Meriwether had shown scientific interests and was intensely concerned with his studies. The President knew Lewis had entered the army and had seen wilderness service on the frontier. The very man to lead the expedition!

Though President Jefferson did not know quite where Captain Lewis might be found at this time, the War Department knew exactly. The captain was an army paymaster at Detroit, then a village deep in the wilderness. In order to pay the troops, Captain Lewis had to travel from one fort to another, mostly in a 21-foot bateau (the craft used by French rivermen) and a 48-foot pirogue (a "dugout" canoe, made by hollowing out a big log), constantly alert for Indians and robbers, since he carried government money with him. Better training for an explorer one could not imagine, for this was just the manner in which the expedition would have to travel.

In March of 1801, Captain Lewis had reached the army quartermaster depot in Pittsburgh, after one of his long wilderness journeys. Here he learned for the first time that his friend Mr. Jefferson had just been elected President of the United States. There was a letter waiting for him, too. Rather astonished, he saw that it was from the President. He was a great deal more surprised when he read it. President Jefferson wanted Captain Lewis to come to Washington at once, to live at the White House as his private secretary — exciting news for an ambitious young officer, but the message Lewis could read between the lines was more exciting still.

Mr. Jefferson was a veteran diplomat. He knew well enough that official letters might be secretly opened and read by unauthorized persons. He dared not mention the expedition, which was still a secret, but he contrived to give Lewis some

hints only he would understand. He wanted Lewis as his secretary, Mr. Jefferson wrote, because he could "contribute to the mass of information which it is interesting for the administration to acquire."

What information *could* a young infantry officer possibly give the President of the United States? Mr. Jefferson gave a few more hints. Again he used words Lewis could understand perfectly, although they would mean little to anyone else. He wanted Lewis as his secretary because of his knowledge of "the Western country."

It was fortunate that President Jefferson did take this precaution, because in order to locate Lewis he had found it necessary to send his letter through the hands of the commander-in-chief, General James Wilkinson. Although President Jefferson did not know it, Wilkinson had for years been a spy in Spanish pay. Thanks to Jefferson's ruse, Wilkinson never guessed what the letter really implied.

Young Captain Lewis realized what the President meant. He knew perfectly well that the job as "secretary" was a mere blind. He himself had no special qualifications as a secretary. For one thing, he could scarcely spell. He knew President Jefferson was not really looking for a secretarial assistant. Plainly this was the transcontinental exploration scheme. Jefferson wanted his young neighbor to join the great adventure. Meriwether Lewis may already have guessed that he was to command it.

He rushed his reply accepting Mr. Jefferson's offer, and a few days later was on his way, riding one horse and leading two more loaded with his baggage. The White House was his destination!

For the next two or three years young Meriwether Lewis lived with the President, who treated him as "one of my family." Since Jefferson was now a widower his household was small, and his secretary a constant companion. The President returned to his beloved Albemarle County as often as possible, and Lewis was sometimes able to visit his own home, only a few miles distant from Jefferson's "Monticello." He handled confidential missions and messages for Jefferson, and had the use of a slave and a horse at the President's personal expense.

The President and his young companion must have had long discussions concerning the whole great project during long evenings together in the White House. Jefferson must have made his decision on the choice of a leader soon after Lewis reached Washington (if not before), since the young officer was almost immediately busy with preparations. By February of 1803, he had learned enough navigation to fix latitude and longitude — a subject usually reserved for naval officers. He was already trying to find and employ an Indian interpreter, although there were so many Indian languages that no one man could possibly speak them all. He was studying to improve an army officer's limited technical training. Soon he was supervising construction of a collapsible iron framework for a river boat, buying medicines, and collecting scientific equipment.

The expedition would need another officer. If Lewis were killed by a grizzly bear (as he very nearly was) or shot by Indians (he once actually felt the wind of an Indian bullet, whizzing just above his head) or trampled to death by a buffalo bull (a big one just missed trampling him in his tent one night) or bitten by a rattlesnake (another near-tragedy), there would have to be some one else to assume command at once.

The President left this important choice to Lewis, whose thoughts turned at once to a tall, red-haired former army officer living on a

William Clark

Kentucky plantation called "Mulberry Hill," near present-day Louisville. This was First Lieutenant William Clark, in whose company Lewis had served as an ensign (as second lieutenants were called in those days). "Billy" Clark's red hair was regarded as a good omen by the Clark family, for it was tradition that all redheaded Clarks eventually distinguished themselves. There may have been truth in this family fable; for not only did William Clark, explorer of the Northwest, have blazing red hair, but so too did his elder brother, General George Rogers Clark, who in the Revolution drove the British out of the land that is today Ohio, Indiana, Illinois, and parts of Wisconsin and Michigan. Without redheaded William Clark the United States might never have extended to the Pacific. Without redheaded George Rogers Clark the Canadian border might today have been on the Ohio River.

Though both William Clark and Meriwether Lewis had been too young to fight in the Revolution, they had both seen active duty — Clark as an officer in the post-Revolutionary Indian fighting in Ohio and Indiana, Lewis in the "Whiskey Rebellion," when President Washington had found it necessary to send troops against farmers in western Pennsylvania who refused to pay the federal tax on whiskey. After hostilities in Pennsylvania were over, Lewis had served briefly in the rifle company that Clark, though only a first lieutenant. had commanded. Lewis knew Clark to be a brave, vigorous, and resourceful man, an experienced woodsman who had spent years in the wildest kind of country. Best of all, he could draw fairly well and would be able to make the maps of the new and unknown West which the explorers were instructed to bring home from their expedition.

President Jefferson approved at once of Lewis's choice, for he had known the Clark family for years. In fact, they had at one time been his Albemarle County neighbors, living on a plantation that directly adjoined Mr. Jefferson's "Monticello."

Lewis wrote Clark from Washington, on June 19, 1803, asking him to accompany the expedition, and adding President Jefferson's "anxious wish that you would consent to join me in this enterprise."

When on July 16, 1803, William Clark received his friend's letter, he took it to General George Rogers Clark, who had received a similar offer from Mr. Jefferson himself twenty years before, and who now urged his younger brother to accept.

"A fine field was open for the display of genius," said the general. William Clark replied next day accepting, and, as Lewis had suggested, began at once to search for young and vigorous- men accustomed to the woods and not afraid of hardship. He particularly wanted hunters. They would have to be skillful, for the explorers would have to depend for meat on the game they killed. As it developed, the expedition usually ate four deer, or an elk and a deer, or one whole buffalo during each day of their journey.

Lewis had long since begun to collect supplies: the collapsible boat he himself had designed, rifles, a plentiful supply of ammunition, clothing, presents for the Indians, knives, tomahawks, astronomical instruments, a swivel gun, and an air gun. All the gunpowder was sealed in lead kegs to keep it dry. As the powder in each keg was used, the lead could be melted down into bullets. The swivel gun was a very small cannon, which could be moved by hand into almost any firing position on the gunwale of a boat or the log stockade of a fort. The air gun was meant for

emergencies. If the expedition ran out of gunpowder, there would still be one weapon left to kill game for food.

The real purpose of the expedition still remained a deep secret, even from the deputy quartermaster general at Pittsburgh — where Lewis, on his way to meet Clark, paused for supplies.

From Pittsburgh, the captain proceeded down the Ohio with men he had already selected — seven soldiers and three other young men whom he was testing, plus a river pilot. Partway down the Ohio he added to his party George Drouilliard, a French Canadian who, after years among the Indians, was expert in the sign language, which all Plains tribes understood (though they often could not understand each other's speech).

At "Mulberry Hill," Clark was waiting; and, on October 26, 1803, the two explorers were off to St. Louis, the Rockies, the Pacific Coast, wild Indians, buffalo country, adventure, danger — and fame.

One member of the group that traveled down the Ohio with Captain Meriwether Lewis is not so famous today as he should be, but he was an interesting and useful member of the exploring party, all the same. This was the captain's faithful Newfoundland dog, Scannon — "active, strong and docile," said Lewis — who shared his master's adventures all the way to the Pacific Coast and back again.

Captain Lewis had paid twenty dollars for him, an enormous price for a dog in those days, and even when a Shawnee Indian, who had never seen such a magnificent creature, offered the larger price of three beaver pelts to buy him, the explorer refused to part with his friend Scannon.

The big dog proved his usefulness to the expedition from the very start. As his master's boat floated down the Ohio on its way to the Mississippi and St. Louis, large numbers of squirrels were seen swimming across the river. Scannon, leaping into the stream, swam after them, killed a number, and, like the good dog he was, brought them dutifully to his master, who had them fried.

It was the Newfoundland's first — but not his last — service to the Lewis and Clark expedition.

From December until May the expedition camped at Rivière du Bois, now called Wood River, near St. Louis, but on the east bank of the Mississippi (since there had not yet been a formal transfer of upper Louisiana to the United States). Clark stayed in camp most of the time, directing the men who were building boats and getting everything prepared for the start.

This left Lewis free to move about neighboring army posts, looking for qualified enlisted men. He found two stalwarts in his own old regiment, a company of which happened to be stationed in Illinois. One was Sergeant John Ordway, a sturdy, trustworthy New Hampshire Yankee. The other was Patrick Gass, an old Indian fighting regular whom the Clark family had known for years. "Paddy" Gass was just what the explorers wanted, for not only was he an experienced soldier, he was also a first-class carpenter, who would be useful in working on the new boats and in helping to build the forts and cabins which the expedition would need when it went into winter quarters. Patrick was small in stature, standing only five feet seven, but he was powerfully built and fearless. When his company commander refused to release so useful a soldier, Gass slipped off privately to join Lewis, who displayed special authority from President Jefferson. So Gass accompanied the expedition!

President Jefferson, who had for years been collecting as much information as possible about the unknown country now lying before them, forwarded one or two maps and some notes. The explorers had at least one other map. A Scotsman who had explored for the Spanish informed Clark on many details concerning the western regions. More facts were gained from rivermen who had been a few hundred miles up the Missouri.

There was a curious tangle of red tape over the rank Clark was to have. Lewis, who had once been his subordinate, was now a Regular Army captain. Clark had been only a first lieutenant when he resigned from the army, and now the War Department suddenly refused to give him the captaincy he had been promised. This was embarrassing for Lewis, who had assured his friend (and former commander) that they were to share the command as equals. Both were embarrassed but they settled the difficulty easily. When they went up the Missouri River, they shared the command, and their men, who thought they were both captains, were never informed of the difference in rank.

It is an army proverb that there must be *one* commander. Command is supposed to be something two men cannot share. But Lewis and Clark were two Regular Army men who did share command in complete equality and with perfect success. They equipped, trained, and disciplined their expedition. They led it successfully across some of the most dangerous country in the world and led it back with equal success, with the loss of but one man — and he died of disease.

There was never any dissension between the two friends. On only two questions did they ever disagree: the desirability of dog meat for dinner and the necessity of salt. When the crisis arose which meant "eat dog or starve," Lewis thought it wasn't really too bad — better than horse, in any case. Clark ate it because he had to, but he disliked it intensely. The expedition ran out of salt on its way across the continent and later had to boil sea water from the Pacific to get a new supply. Tasting salt once more, Lewis thought it was a "great treat." Clark said it was a mere "matter of indifference."

Except for these two small differences of opinion, all was harmony. Through the blazing heat of the midsummer plains and the freezing cold of the Rockies, the two led their men to the Pacific and returned in perfect agreement. They remained friends to the end of their lives.

2

EVERYTHING WAS READY for the start by Sunday, May 13, 1804, but the boats did not actually push off until the next day. The permanent party consisted, at the beginning, of thirty-two men. In addition to these, seven United States Army soldiers and ten St. Louis boatmen were to accompany the expedition on the first leg of its journey. Though the explorers sooner or later would have to rely on hunting for survival, they set out with a large reserve of food — 14 barrels of "parch meal" made of corn, 20 barrels of flour, 50 kegs of pork, and 7 barrels of salt. The expedition also had one unusual piece of equipment. Private Peter Cruzat took his violin along, and played it, for occasional dancing, all the way across the continent. No hardships ever completely dis-

couraged these men, so long as they could dance (without even having girls for their partners) to Cruzat's lively fiddle.

Clark started with the boats while Lewis was still completing a last-minute visit to St. Louis. It was easy to catch up by riding overland. The two captains were together again at St. Charles on May 20, and the boats moved upriver on May 21. The first few hundred miles of the journey were not especially dangerous, though forcing the boats against the swift Missouri current was al-

ways hard work. Often the men had to abandon sails and oars and take the cordelle (towrope), to haul their craft upstream, struggling through mud, wading in the water, clambering over boulders.

The sergeants each assumed special duties. One took the helm of the big keelboat. Another kept a sharp lookout from the bow for snags in the river, for signals from officers, or from their hunters ashore. A third, commanding a small guard, watched from the boat itself by day, posted sentries when the expedition camped, and, several times each night, scouted the area around the camp for possible Indian raiders.

The hunters at first killed so many deer that the men, with more than they could eat, began to jerk (that is, dry) venison for a food reserve. As yet there were no buffalo or Indians, but signs of both soon began to appear.

Near the present border between South Dakota and Nebraska, on June 12, 1804, the expedition met white men, descending the Missouri on two rafts. Among them they found the veteran frontiersman, Pierre Dorion, who at one time had corresponded with George Rogers Clark. While they camped together that night, the captains, listening to Dorion's description of the country upstream, realized that chance had sent them the very man they needed. Dorion, who had lived for twenty years among the Sioux, would be a valuable interpreter at councils with the tribe; and he might be able to induce some of the chiefs to visit the city of Washington, as President Jefferson wished. Lewis and Clark persuaded Dorion to return upstream with them as far as the Sioux country.

Before reaching the hunting grounds of the Sioux, however, they paused at the mouth of the Platte River to make friends with the Oto, Maha, and Missouri tribes; and here they had serious disciplinary problems within their own ranks. Trouble of this sort had commenced before the expedition had left camp near St. Louis, for not all of these men were trained soldiers, accustomed to military discipline. Some of the men had been recruited mainly as hunters. These adventurers were wild, free spirits, with no intention of obeying orders. One man refused to mount guard in obedience to a sergeant's orders. Just before leaving the white settlements, others had misbehaved at a ball. Later some of the men broke into the expedition's stock of whiskey and got roaring drunk. Once, a sentry fell asleep on guard — an offense for which he could lawfully have been put to death. There was a series of courts-martial to deal with these offenses.

When the expedition paused to council with

the Otos on the Platte River, two men deserted, one a soldier, the other an *engagé*, that is, a hired civilian riverman. Suspecting both were hiding in the Oto village, Lewis and Clark sent Drouilliard to bring them back, dead or alive. With three soldiers to help him, Drouilliard captured both, but the *engagé* escaped and could not be recaptured. The soldier was court-martialed and sentenced to run the gantlet four times, through the ranks of his fellow soldiers, each armed with a bundle of switches. The Oto chiefs, whom Drouilliard had brought to confer with Lewis and Clark, were horrified to witness such a punishment; for, however cruel Indians might be at times, they did not believe in whipping (although some tribes did make their captives run the gantlet).

Lewis realized that this was an unfavorable beginning for a conference with the Otos and took the necessary time to explain army discipline. Eventually he convinced the chiefs that he was being just in his punishment. Officers and chiefs then held a council. Like most of the powwows Lewis and Clark later held with other tribes, this was mainly an effort to help the Indians understand that the United States was taking possession of the Louisiana Purchase and that French and Spanish control had ended. Although it was impossible to make the redskins fully comprehend what had happened far away in Paris, the white leaders did the best they could. They explained that they came from "the Great Chief of the Seventeen great nations of America" (there were then only seventeen states in the Union) to tell his red children of a "council" he had held with their "old fathers," the French and Spanish. The great American chief, Thomas Jefferson, now controlled the rivers, and his American traders would soon bring white man's goods for the Indians to buy — a matter of great importance to all the tribes. He would like the Oto chiefs to come to Washington and council with him. Then the explorers did some shooting with the air gun (which always astonished Indians) and gave everyone a drink.

Two days later, as the expedition moved on up

the Missouri, came its first and only tragedy. Sergeant Floyd was stricken with what the Lewis and Clark Journals call a "bilious cholic" (which may have been appendicitis); and though his comrades did all they could for him, the poor fellow grew steadily weaker, dying as they approached what is now Sioux City, Iowa. His fellow explorers paused to dig a grave, fitting oak slabs about Floyd's body to protect it, fired the army's traditional salute to a dead soldier over the grave, and went on.

Presently there was another case of bad discipline. Private John Newman spoke mutinously to Captain Lewis, was instantly arrested, and that night went before a court-martial, which sentenced him to seventy-five lashes and dismissal from the permanent exploration party. He had to remain with the other men, since there was no place to confine him; but he was to be sent back to the United States in disgrace with the return party the following spring. Arikara Indians, who saw the seventy-five lashes administered, were as shocked as the Oto chiefs had been. Never, they told the white men, did they whip anyone — not even naughty children.

Newman's was the last offense. There were no more courts-martial, for by this time the captains' firmness had established a proper standard of discipline. During the next two years, through danger, hardship, hunger, and incredible effort, the men of the expedition were obedient, willing, loyal. Poor Newman, repentant, tried hard throughout the following winter to make amends for what he had done; but both he and the deserter Reed were to be dismissed and sent back in the spring. Mutiny and desertion were offenses too serious to condone.

The expedition was soon having so much friction with Sioux Indians that all other troubles were forgotten. The Sioux were a fierce, proud race of magnificent Indians, brave and intelligent though cruel — haughty lords of the buffalo lands, who in those days could not imagine any nation mightier than their own. Lewis and Clark were not the last white men to have trouble with them. The tribe was not finally subdued until long after the Civil War.

On August 27, their first Sioux was sighted swimming out toward the boats; and, as the craft turned shoreward, two more appeared. When Pierre Dorion, chatting with them, learned that there were large Sioux camps just ahead, he and one of the French *engagés* went overland to invite the chiefs to a friendly council.

Dorion soon returned with his son, whom he

had found in the village, and with five chiefs — not to mention some seventy uninvited boys and warriors (who came along out of sheer curiosity). These Indians, the explorers thought, were "stout bold looking people," wearing leather clothing much embroidered with colored porcupine quills, which Indians used for decoration before they were able to buy bright glass beads from white traders. Only a few had rifles, the rest carrying bows and arrows; for the prairie tribes of the upper Missouri River had such limited contacts with white men that firearms and ammunition were hard to obtain.

Formally raising the American flag, the captains began the council. Lewis made approximately the same speech he had made to the Otos and would be making to Indian gatherings all the way across the continent. The Sioux, he said, were now under the protection of the Great White Father in Washington, who wished them to keep the peace and would soon send traders. The prospect of more traders was what really interested the Sioux, who greatly desired white men's wares, for which they had many buffalo robes to offer in exchange.

All the chiefs were presented with medals, specially struck for the expedition, which showed President Jefferson's portrait on one side and on the other a crossed tomahawk and peace pipe, with two hands clasped in friendship. The grand chief was given a United States artillery uniform coat of army blue with red facings and much gold lace, an officer's cocked hat, an American flag, and an "Indian commission" (an official paper, signed by Lewis and Clark in the name of the President, certifying that the chief who carried it was to be treated as a friend and ally of the United States).

The chiefs now retired to a leafy bower, which the younger Sioux had built for them, to confer among themselves and to prepare their reply. Meanwhile the white men entertained the remaining Indians at a bow-and-arrow shooting match. The prizes were blue beads. After this, the young warriors painted themselves and danced to divert their visitors.

Next morning the chiefs sat down in a dignified row, with their peace pipes pointing to special places of honor for the two captains. The grand chief promised peace. Pierre Dorion was to be left with them, and in the spring Sioux chiefs would go with him to visit the Great White Father in Washington. Other chiefs, in their speeches, asked for traders to be sent to the Sioux country bringing ammunition, domestic goods that their squaws could use, and "milk of the great father" — which meant whiskey. With their councils ended (successfully, as they thought) Lewis and Clark went on up the river, leaving Dorion behind to escort the Sioux chiefs to Washington.

On that very day, as Lewis and Clark met in conference with the Sioux, a sea captain in far-off Massachusetts was unintentionally preparing the greatest disappointment of this western journey. Captain Samuel Hill was sailing the brig *Lydia* out of Boston harbor on his way to the Pacific Coast and the mouth of the Columbia River, whither the Lewis and Clark expedition was bound overland — and where they hoped to find an American ship to take them home. Would they make connections or wouldn't they? Only the future could tell, but the party was prepared to return overland if necessary.

The expedition still possessed two horses, which, since they could not be transported in the boats, had to be ridden or led along the bank of the river. Private George Shannon — the youngest member of the expedition, in fact hardly more than a boy — had been sent ahead with these animals. He had been ordered to keep in touch with the boats, but while the captains paused for their council with the Sioux, he had forged too far ahead. For a week there was no trace of Shannon. A special landing party could not find him. A man sent to search the nearby prairies returned unsuccessful. Everyone was now alarmed. Shannon had expected to be separated from the others only a short time and had taken very little food and ammunition. He would not be able to kill much game for himself. A third searching party, carrying extra provisions, went out to seek him, but no one could find Shannon.

It was a great relief when one day they saw a young white man ride down the bank of the Missouri — Shannon, at last! After using all his bullets, he had survived for twelve days, mostly on wild grapes. He still had powder, and he had whittled a wooden bullet, with which he had managed to kill one rabbit. As he grew weaker, he had turned one of the horses loose on the prairie, keeping the other to ride (and perhaps to eat, if worse came to worst). Believing he would never find his comrades again, he had camped by the river, hoping some white trader's boat might by chance come by.

Other men were sent ashore to care for Shannon's horse, now the only draft animal they were sure they possessed. Indians soon stole it, however. Fortunately the experienced Drouilliard scoured the prairies till he found the second horse, which Shannon had turned loose.

Thus far, although they felt certain more Sioux were somewhere near, the explorers had seen only those with whom they had held council. Now, as more Indians began to appear along shore in small groups, they learned that two villages of Teton Sioux (one division of the great Sioux nation) were a short distance up the river — one camp of eighty tepees and one of sixty. This meant nearly 1500 redskins and, council or no council, Lewis and Clark were by no means sure they would be friendly.

The two leading chiefs in these villages were men of contrasting character. One, Black Buffalo (or Black Buffalo Bull) was farseeing enough to know that it would pay to treat the white men well. The other, the Partizan, was a brutal, greedy, and violent man who proved unfriendly from the first, probably because he hoped to frighten the new arrivals into giving him unusually large presents.

Since leaving Dorion (who spoke excellent Sioux) behind, they had no interpreter except one *engagé*, far less fluent in the language. The explorers therefore did not try to hold another council, but invited the leading warriors aboard the boats, to see the air gun and other curiosities, and to have a little whiskey. They were careful not

to give the Indians more than a quarter of a glass apiece. But, after the Sioux had gulped even one drink, it was hard to speed these thirsty guests ashore again. And, when Clark took presents ashore for the others, three young Indians held the rope of his pirogue, refusing to let him return to the other boats. The Partizan, pretending to be drunk, jostled him roughly.

Soon it appeared there might be a fight with the growing mob of surly Indians. Clark with redheaded courage drew his sword, and the three men with him prepared for action. Lewis, seeing the trouble ashore, ordered the party in the boats to grab their guns, and himself manned the swivel. The warriors, with bows already strung, began to jerk arrows from their quivers. Getting the pirogue loose at last, Clark sent it out to Lewis, who returned in this craft with twelve soldiers. They paddled ashore to reinforce Clark and his men.

Seeing these reinforcements arriving, all armed with rifles against mere arrows, the Sioux faltered. Doubtless they felt the usual Indian fear of artillery as they viewed the swivel gun aimed in their direction and ready to fire. Many of the warriors began to disappear, leaving the chiefs behind. Though the Partizan was still in an ugly mood, Black Buffalo took the situation firmly in hand. Clark offered to shake hands with both chiefs. Both refused, but as the boat moved away Black Buffalo and three warriors waded after it and to the white men's surprise climbed aboard in a perfectly friendly way — eager, apparently, to accompany the white men on the next short leg of the journey.

The expedition pushed on about a mile, to camp on an island where the water would help protect them from a possible attack. On the previous evening, they had camped on an island that Clark named Good Humored Island, because everyone was in fine spirits. Now, with everyone irritated, he named the new camping ground Bad Humored Island. But, with the river all around them and an alert guard, the explorers and the four friendly Sioux slept in safety and next morning pushed on upstream with no additional trouble, though the banks for four miles were crowded with Sioux, no longer actively hostile but merely curious.

At the next Indian village Captain Lewis, taking a few soldiers, went ashore with Black Buffalo and his Indian companions. These braves seemed to be devoted family men who wanted their squaws and children to see the strangers. When the young co-leader had not returned after three hours, Clark became anxious and sent a sergeant to see what was happening ashore. Word came back that all these Sioux seemed friendly.

Then Clark, too, went ashore. Both officers, the tall redheaded Clark and the tall blond and blue-eyed Lewis, were placed on an ornamented buffalo robe — a special mark of honor — and solemnly carried to the council. This conference

was followed by a feast, a dance, and yet another dance on the following day. But some Maha Indian prisoners whispered that in spite of all this show of friendship the Sioux intended to stop the white men; and the Partizan, who now reappeared, began to stir up new animosity.

When the expedition was ready to leave this village and move on, several warriors used the now well-known device of grasping the cable of the boat, demanding presents of tobacco. Lewis was ready to slash the cable with his sword but Clark handed some tobacco to Black Buffalo, who passed it on to the greedy warriors and again got into the boat with the white men. After that, though Indians continued to appear along the bank, there was no hostility.

Presently, after smoking the pipe of peace and receiving presents, Black Buffalo was ready to depart, assuring the white men that from this point on they would see no more Sioux.

On October 8, 1804, Lewis and Clark came to the lower of the three villages of the Arikaras, or "Rickarees." The Sioux they had met were prairie nomads, living in conical tepees of buffalo hide that could be moved from place to place as their whims might dictate. The Arikaras — like the Mandans, farther up the Missouri — lived in permanent towns, with big round houses made of logs, covered with woven willow branches, dry grass, and a thick coating of earth. Around the villages were fields of corn, beans, and a plant used instead of tobacco. Arikaras could smoke it; white men who tried to usually wished they hadn't.

Going ashore, Lewis soon came back with two French-Canadian traders, Pierre-Antoine Tabeau and his assistant, Joseph Gravelines. Since Tabeau was living in the lodge of Kakawita, the local chief, and since he and Gravelines both spoke Arikara, there was no difficulty getting along with these Indians. The presence of Clark's Negro slave York was a big help, for York astonished the Arikaras, who had never seen a black man in their lives. At first, like so many other Indians, they suspected the Negro was not really black but only painted. York, who was himself much amused, explained to the Indians that he was really a wild animal and that Captain Clark had caught and tamed him.

After the way the Sioux had treated them, the explorers found Arikara cordiality a delightful contrast. Because Tabeau had quietly warned them that the various chiefs might become jealous of each other, Lewis and Clark tactfully invited leaders of all three villages to the same council. Afterward they took the chiefs of the upper villages aboard and went to visit each of their towns. Two unusual things happened among the Arikaras. Instead of begging for tobacco, these Indians gave the white men some of their own smoking mixture. They also refused liquor, of which most Indians were dangerously fond. Drink, said the wise Arikara warriors, made a man a fool.

THEIR NEXT STOP, as the explorers realized, would be a big Mandan village fifty or sixty miles up the Missouri from what is now Bismarck, North Dakota. There they would spend the winter. To promote peace between this tribe and the Arikaras, they took with them an Arikara chief as a sort of intertribal ambassador.

Altogether there were five Mandan villages, very much like those of the Arikaras, with similar large, circular earth houses. Mandan council houses, built in this way, could accommodate as many as 200 warriors, and even the dwellings of individual tribesmen might be fifty feet in diameter, bigger than many modern houses.

Not far from the Mandans lived other tribes the most important being the Minnetarees, who had two villages of their own; and there was also a small village of Wetersoon. All these Indians were on friendly terms with each other. And so many traders from Canada had visited them that they had long since learned the commercial advantages of being friendly toward white men.

While awaiting Clark, who was bringing the boats up the river, Lewis made visits to neighboring villages. From the first Mandan village two chiefs went overland with Lewis to the next one. When Clark arrived he had with him a Canadian, René Jussome, who had been living among these Indians for fifteen years. Jussome was exactly the man needed to interpret, especially as he knew all the peculiarities of the local chiefs, with whom Lewis and Clark would have to deal. This was important, since the powerful one-eyed chieftain Kakoakis was a huge and brutal fellow who privately despised his American visitors. Worse still, he also despised the friendly Mandan chief, She-he-ke (usually known as "The Big White," because of his light complexion) and had probably had friction with Poscopsahe (Black Cat), supreme chief of the Mandans. Black Cat, friendly from the beginning, guided the two officers to a likely spot for their winter fort, but, since timber at that location was scarce, they finally chose another.

Though delayed by high winds (which at first made it impossible for several important chiefs to join them by crossing the wild Missouri) Lewis and Clark's eventual council with the Mandans and their neighbors was a great success. A second Arikara chief also attended, to help make peace between the two tribes. Various important Indians received American flags, and military coats, while the grand chief in each village received one of President Jefferson's medals. One Indian was given a silver dollar, which he could not possibly spend so far from any trading post, but which he could use as an impressive decoration. One or two chiefs, suspecting the medals were "bad medicine" — some kind of malicious magic — soon passed them along to other Indians who were less suspicious. As was customary, the council adjourned to give the chiefs time to deliberate privately over what they had heard.

Before the council could meet once more, the explorers saw for the first time the grandeur and horror of a prairie fire. The grass, which grew several feet high on the prairies, was now so dry that a spark was enough to set it ablaze. Lightning, a hunter careless with his campfire, or warriors making smoke signals might start a prairie fire at any time. In a high wind such a conflagration would sweep forward through the tall, dry grass in a towering wall of flame that could not be stopped, sometimes moving so swiftly that the people caught before it could not escape. In a matter of minutes a thousand acres might be a roaring inferno, the wind driving sparks forward to kindle new fires far ahead. Often a blaze like this could be seen for forty miles. "The flame at one moment curls along the ground," said one early traveler, "and seems to lick up its fuel from below, while at the next it tumbles over like breakers of the sea upon the dried grass, and sweeps it in a wave of fire from the ground."

In the fire that Lewis and Clark witnessed, two

Indians died and three had serious burns. One boy was saved only because his mother threw a raw buffalo hide over him, with its moist, untanned side uppermost. The fire swept quickly over the boy, burning neither him nor the grass around him under the robe.

The second council was a triumph for the American effort to maintain amity among the In-

dian tribes. The Mandans and the Minnetarees agreed to make peace with the Arikaras, and sent delegations to the Arikara villages to council with them.

On November 3 the exploring party set to work building winter quarters. The health of many of the men had been undermined by the long, hard journey in constant dampness. During the last few weeks cold weather had increased their hardships. Clark and two others had begun to suffer from rheumatism. Lewis had been poisoned by minerals in the water. There had been an epidemic of boils and abscesses, due to the men's exhaustion. They all needed a long rest in warm, dry cabins before spring arrived, when they would set off again on the hardest part of their journey, through the mysterious regions that still lay ahead.

Although the prairies themselves were treeless, it was always possible to find timber along the river bottoms, soft wood, but good enough to build cabins that would need to last only one winter. Sergeant "Paddy" Gass, the former carpenter, was exactly the man the expedition needed now. Clark, despite his rheumatism, directed the building while Lewis, who was the scientific observer of the party, sat writing the expedition's records. René Jussome and his family moved in with the other cabin dwellers, so that he would always be on hand to interpret — a major reason why pleasant relations with the Indians lasted throughout the winter. Some of the civilian *engagés,* who were not expected to go farther, began to build a boat for their return journey.

Although the Indians had been friendly thus far, there was no point in taking chances. Redskins were a changeable people, and no one could predict when their friendly mood would alter. During Wayne's Indian campaign, Clark had learned the value of building secure fortifications against surprise attacks. He meant to protect his men by making them just as secure as Wayne's had been. The expedition's winter quarters were designed to be a small fort, shaped like a slice of pie. The strong walls of the log cabins formed two sides, joining at an acute angle. Across the base of this triangle ran a stout log palisade, slightly curved.

By mid-November, the cabins had been erected and the men could begin "dobing" them. It was never possible to make rough-hewn logs fit tightly together, as modern sawed lumber does. But mud, "dobed" into the chinks, shut out the cold and made the cabins tight and warm. Instead of the dirt floor of many frontier log cabins, these

boasted the added luxury of puncheon floors —
split logs laid flat side up.

While everyone was busily at work on these
tasks, a new arrival who was to become one of
the most famous members of the Lewis and Clark
expedition walked quietly into its camp. The date
was November 11, 1804. This was a young Indian
girl, Sacagawea, one of the two Shoshone wives
of a white man named Toussaint Charbonneau,
who had been living among the Indians for ten
years (half of this time among the Minnetarees).

The distant Shoshone tribe, to which Sacagawea
belonged, were Rocky Mountain Indians living
near the headwaters of the Missouri River. When
she had been scarcely more than a child,
Sacagawea had been captured by a raiding party
of Minnetarees. The warrior who owned her had
gambled her away to Charbonneau, who kept
her for one of his wives.

As they came to know Sacagawea and Charbonneau, Lewis and Clark realized that these two
would be invaluable on the next leg of their westward journey. Though Charbonneau was a rather

worthless fellow, he knew Indian languages; and when the expedition reached the Rockies they certainly would need a Shoshone interpreter like Sacagawea. For one thing they would have to find pack horses to carry the baggage over the mountains, and these they could get only from the Shoshones. Sacagawea would be of enormous value in bargaining for the animals on which the entire success of the expedition would depend. Eventually Charbonneau agreed to go, although since the expedition could not take two squaws along he would have to leave his other wife behind.

In February, 1805, Sacagawea had a baby boy. She had a harder time in labor than most Indian women, and the two captains tried to give medical aid. Any frontier army officer in those days was more or less accustomed to doctoring his men, and Lewis had learned a good deal about medicine from his mother. But neither Lewis nor Clark knew much about obstetrics. While they were wondering what to do, René Jussome told them that a powder made from the rattle of a rattlesnake sometimes helped in difficult childbirth. Lewis, always interested in acquiring biological specimens, happened to have a rattle with him. Jussome broke off two of the rings, which he crushed in water. Ten minutes after Sacagawea had taken a dose of the supposed remedy, her baby was safely delivered. This, of course, was pure coincidence. The "medicine" had nothing to do with the birth, but at least mother and child were safe, and soon doing well.

Most people have a mistaken idea of the sort of assistance Sacagawea actually gave the Lewis and Clark expedition. This is a pity, for it spoils the real story of a very brave and fine Indian girl. It has often been said that she "guided Lewis and Clark across the continent." That is obviously nonsense. Except over a very small part of the distance, the Shoshone girl knew nothing about the Lewis and Clark route. Like most Indians, she was acquainted only with a comparatively limited area in which her own band wandered. Besides, for most of their journey Lewis and Clark had no need for any guide. As long as they were on the Missouri River, all they had to do was keep going upstream. When much later they reached the Columbia, they needed only to keep floating downstream until they reached the Pacific Ocean. The critical moment came when the explorers were between the headwaters of the two rivers, divided by the Rockies. Here the expedition had to get pack horses — or fail. And it was here that Sacagawea saved them. She did not guide them, but without her assistance the Lewis and Clark expedition might never have secured the horses on which success depended.

Judged by the customary life on the frontier, the winter of 1804–1805 was peaceful and pleasant. Canadian traders, coming overland from Canada, were somewhat disgruntled to find United States Army forces among the Mandan Indians, but they made no serious trouble. The captains worked at their records, observed the Indians, and collected vocabularies of their languages — in which Mr. Jefferson was much interested. They had brought along printed lists of English words with blank spaces opposite each word for its equivalent in the languages of various Indian tribes. These spaces they filled whenever possible. Clark was busy working up his rough topographical notes into more finished maps of the country, the first maps of these areas ever made. Both officers and some of the men kept diaries.

The Negro York continued to be a great curiosity to the Indians. The chief Kakoakis (One Eye) paid a special visit to the fort to inquire about a story "some foolish young men" had told him. They said the Americans had with them a man who was neither red nor white but black — all over. Could this possibly be true? When York appeared, the skeptical chief, like many other Indians, moistened a fingertip and tried to rub off the color!

The Mandans and Minnetarees, though sometimes suspicious, were generally hospitable throughout the winter. The Indian girls were far too friendly — so much so that some of the red warriors were jealous. The only real "Indian trouble" was with a war party of Sioux and

Pawnees, against whom the Americans turned out to help their Mandan friends, although the raiders disappeared so swiftly that there was no fighting. Buffalo beef was usually plentiful; but, occasionally, when the herds had moved, hunters out on the prairies found game scarce and food difficult to obtain. One hunting party of three men had nothing but a wolf to eat during three hungry days.

On Christmas Day, 1804, the lonely little group of white men held a celebration of their own. Indians, who usually swarmed around the fort, were asked not to come on that day, which was reserved as "great medicine" for white men. The Christmas celebration began in the morning with a volley of rifle fire and a salute from the swivel, followed by a round of brandy. The expedition raised the American flag. Some of the men went hunting. Others cleared a cabin floor and had a dance to the music of Cruzat's violin. The only ladies present were the two Madames Charbonneau and Madame Jussome, all three of them squaws who did not understand the white men's dances and merely watched. Americans in those days knew only square dances, so they managed very well without feminine partners.

Christmas dinner was as luxurious a feast as their scanty store made possible — bread baked from real wheat flour (no cornmeal), dried apples, and even pepper, all rarities on the prairie. The swivel was fired again at half past two as the signal for another dance. And the celebration continued until eight o'clock in the evening, which everyone regarded as an alarmingly late hour.

New Year's Day was just such another festive occasion, with more salutes and rum. Later in the morning Captain Clark stood drinks all round, and in the afternoon Captain Lewis stood another round. Then off they went to the Mandans, marching into the village to the music of Cruzat's violin, a tambourine, and a "sounden horn" (which must have been the expedition's bugle), and going gaily from one lodge to another for more dancing.

THE SPRING of 1805, when it came at last, brought buffalo, floating and whirling, alive or dead, among the cakes of ice rushing down the Missouri. This saved the Indians the trouble of hunting. Leaping from one ice cake to another, the Mandans brought in the carcasses, not caring in the least — as the white men observed with disgust — how long the animals had been dead. To the Indians, meat was meat, no matter what its state of preservation, for they really enjoyed buffalo beef when it was rather "high."

Spring meant that it would soon be time for the Americans to start westward, on the really perilous part of their journey, into lands white men had never visited, and through these mountainous regions to the Pacific Coast (where American sailors had long been trading). The explorers had repaired their boats during the winter and had constructed several new ones. Traders in the villages would soon be on their way back to Canada, while the expedition's *engagés,* and a few of the soldiers, would be sent home.

Corporal Richard Warfington took command of this homeward-bound party. The corporal himself had a good record and was being sent back only because his enlistment had expired. The *engagés* had not contracted to go farther. Private Newman, who had long repented his mutinous conduct, pleaded not to be sent home but to be allowed to accompany the westward journey. Captain Lewis sympathized with the man and knew his conduct had been good all winter, but also realized that any soldier once guilty of mutiny is a poor risk. Lewis had to maintain discipline. Newman went home.

It is a tribute to the wisdom of the two commanders that they sifted from among the party exactly the right men for their advance into the unknown western lands. Through all the ensuing dangers and hardships each man of this "Corps of Discovery" did his full duty. There were no more courts-martial and no more floggings on the expedition. Charbonneau, to be sure, made trouble, but only because he was stupid and clumsy. It was possible to tolerate him in view of Sacagawea's aid as an interpreter. Naturally Lewis and Clark, being kindly, humane men let this bright Indian woman bring her baby with her.

The two groups, now parting company, set out in opposite directions about five o'clock on the afternoon of April 7, 1805. Corporal Warfington's pirogue turned down the Missouri, homeward bound. Red-haired Captain Clark, with two large boats and six small canoes turned up the river, while Captain Lewis traveled for a time on foot along the shore.

As the boats launched forth upon the wide Missouri that spring afternoon, neither party could guess that the brig *Lydia* of Boston, the only ship that could possibly take them home by sea, was on that very day putting in to the Columbia

River's mouth quite prematurely after the long voyage around Cape Horn.

The Lewis and Clark expedition almost came to an end not far from the Mandan villages, soon after the resumption of the trip. The near-disaster was the first of a series due to Charbonneau's clumsiness. In spite of the years he had lived along the Missouri, this odd character knew nothing about boats and could not even swim.

May 15, 1805, turned out to be such a beautiful day that both officers left the boats and were traveling along the shore (it was part of their mission to explore the prairies as well as the river). Charbonneau was at the helm of that invaluable boat carrying all the expedition's records and many vital supplies. The prairie winds, sweeping across the river, were already kicking up large waves when a sudden violent gust hit the sail. Instead of letting the boat turn with the wind and run before it, which would have been perfectly safe, Charbonneau turned the boat in such a way that the square sail caught the full blast

of the wind. Instantly the craft heeled far over and began to fill with water. Completely panic-stricken, Charbonneau let go of the helm altogether, leaving the capsizing boat completely out of control.

Lewis and Clark, who could see the whole fiasco from the shore, fired their rifles to attract the men's attention. They tried vainly to shout orders but they could not possibly make their voices heard across the wide stretch of open

river, with the wind and water roaring. In his excitement Lewis dropped his rifle, threw down his shot pouch, and began to unbutton his coat. Then he realized, with despair, that it was certain death to try to swim three hundred yards to the boat through icy water, a swift current, and billowing waves.

It was Cruzat, the fiddler, who saved the endangered craft by threatening to shoot Charbonneau then and there, unless he took the tiller once again. The boat righted itself, almost filling with water but not quite sinking.

Sacagawea, who unlike her husband always seemed to do the right thing at the right time, did not lose her head for an instant. Though she had her helpless baby to protect, she calmly pulled from the river various articles of equipment spilled from the deck as they floated past her. Cruzat ordered two men to bail with all their might, while he and the others maneuvered their waterlogged craft toward the shore, in time to keep it from sinking.

There was nothing to be done but to halt the

entire expedition, make camp, and unload the boat, which carried all the medicines, the precious records, and the scientific instruments without which they could not possibly continue. Only a small part of the equipment was washed from the deck and lost in the river. The quick-witted Shoshone squaw had saved many of the articles that floated. Although some of the medicine was ruined, almost everything else could be dried out and saved. The records had not been under water long enough to ruin them and were so carefully handled and preserved that they can easily be read even today.

Almost as soon as the expedition was able to set off again, a new danger appeared, grizzly bears. As the explorers were now reaching wilder regions, where even Indians did not hunt very frequently, the plains often swarmed with game — antelope, elk, and enormous herds of buffalo. Where there was such plentiful food, grizzly bears were so numerous that one trapper, on a later expedition, counted 220 in a single day.

In our own era, these huge beasts have learned

to flee from the mere scent of human beings, but those which Lewis and Clark encountered had never heard a rifle shot, and had no fear of man whatsoever. These grizzlies knew from experience that it was easier to kill an Indian armed only with bow and arrow than it was for the Indian to kill the grizzly.

Plains grizzlies were enormous creatures of incredible strength, weighing as much as half a ton, swift enough to run down a wild horse. The Spaniards, who sometimes hunted them with lariats, soon found that one bear, roped twice, could still walk off dragging riders and their horses as well.

For the most part, the big animals were not likely to attack anyone so long as they were not disturbed; but, being wholly fearless, they frequently approached too close for the expedition's comfort. This was partly because grizzlies have an insatiable curiosity and partly because the odor of the fresh meat on which the explorers lived attracted them into camp. When a bear came within rifle range, someone inevitably shot at him. Usually, low-powered weapons of those days merely wounded the bear, which promptly attacked, driven frantic by the pain. Several of the men, Captain Lewis included, narrowly escaped death before they learned how to deal with this new and formidable foe.

During their winter with the Mandans, the expedition had been hearing a good many Indian stories about grizzly bears without taking them very seriously. They realized that the animals must be very large from the size of the claws, which a few Indians proudly wore as necklaces; and they knew that grizzlies had killed two Minnetarees during the winter. The bears were so dangerous, said the red warriors, that to kill one was as great an achievement as killing a warrior of a hostile tribe in battle.

The two army officers listened tolerantly, though skeptically. That was all very well for Indians, with nothing better than arrows or the inferior firearms the traders sold them. But United States Army rifles, in the hands of the expedition's skilled marksmen, would make short work of any animal on the prairies, no matter how big or how powerful.

This cheerful delusion lasted only till they met their first grizzly. Soon after leaving winter quarters, they began to see tracks in the sand along the river, especially where there were dead buffalo. The footprints were huge, sometimes eleven inches long and seven and a half inches wide. They all wanted to see the creatures that made them, and a few days later they had their wish when two bears appeared at once, while Lewis and a companion were ashore.

Still confident in the stopping power of army bullets, the two men fired together, thus foolishly emptying both rifles. Luckily, one bear fled. The other charged. Unable to load for second shots, both men had to dodge about to keep away from the bear's quick, violent rushes. If the animal had chased only one man, he would have killed him easily, but the two of them were able to divide the bear's attention long enough to reload their rifles and finally kill him. When the excitement was over, they found this savage creature was nothing but a cub, weighing a mere three hundred pounds.

Not long after, Clark and Drouilliard met a full-grown grizzly that required ten bullets to kill. Though this was an adult bear, it too was a small one, less than nine feet long and weighing only six or seven hundred pounds. It took some days before the Americans learned that only a bullet in the brain would kill a grizzly fast enough to keep him from attacking. Possibly a bullet in the heart would have done just as well, but no one ever achieved such a shot.

A few days later, from the vantage point of one of the boats, Lewis saw a white man running wildly across the prairie, yelling and waving his arms. When they pulled him safely aboard, they found it was Private William Bratton, who after firing at a grizzly, and wounding it, had had to run for his life with an unloaded rifle. The bear had chased him half a mile.

Seven hunters landed and followed the bloody trail. They found the wounded bear, still full of fight.

By this time the white men had learned that grizzly hunters must always keep other hunters in reserve with loaded rifles; but even that was not always a guaranty of safety. Once when a party of six men met a grizzly, four fired and hit him, while the other two held their fire. The bear charged. The men with the loaded rifles then fired also.

Carrying six bullets, the bear still chased the men. All six hunters ran for the river. Two of

The other four, with no chance to reach the
canoe, hid in a cluster of willows, trying to reload.
When the bear started for them, two, still with
empty rifles, jumped over a twenty-foot cliff into
the Missouri. So did the bear, landing with a
mighty splash near one of the frantic swimmers.
Fortunately the bear was downstream from him,
so that the stiff Missouri current was against the
raging animal. While all this was happening, one

of the hunters on the bluff above the river —
perfectly safe now, and able to take cool and careful aim at short range — put an end to the bear
before he could reach the swimming men.

The excitable Charbonneau, when once chased
by a grizzly, lost his head as usual and fired into
the air instead of at the bear. While he hid in
some bushes, Drouilliard saved him with an expert shot.

Meriwether Lewis himself was careless enough
one day to go strolling across the prairies without
reloading his rifle after killing a buffalo. He
turned suddenly to see a grizzly walking toward
him, only twenty paces away. What happened
then shows that there would have been less
danger from grizzlies if the explorers had not
irritated them. Keeping his head, as he always
did, the captain walked slowly toward the nearest
tree, which he knew the grizzly could not climb.

When the bear broke into a run, Lewis decided
against the tree and sprinted for the river, plung-
ing in up to his waist and wading out until the
animal would have to swim to reach him. Then,

turning and facing the bear, he thrust out his espontoon (a kind of spear army officers carried in those days). The bear came down to the shore, looked at the man in the water — then suddenly turned and ran! Scrambling out and reloading, Lewis watched it retreat a good three miles across the open prairie.

His day of adventures was by no means over. On his way back to camp, he met an unknown animal "of the tiger kind," perhaps a mountain lion, fired, missed, but frightened it away. Next morning he awoke to find a rattlesnake coiled in a tree above him.

The big prairie rattlesnakes, sometimes four feet long, were a real danger. No one was bitten, but there were narrow escapes. One man was saved because his heavy leather leggings stopped the deadly fangs. Another, lying down to rest and idly stretching out his hand, brought it down on a rattler's head. He snatched it back in time. A fisherman, standing by the river, glanced down to see a rattlesnake between his feet, but shot the reptile before it could strike. Lewis, hearing a rattle in the dark, killed the unseen snake by slashing with his espontoon, guided only by the sinister sound.

Other animals made trouble, accidentally. A buffalo, swimming the Missouri one night, made the mistake of trying to scramble out on a boat moored along the bank, then, frightened, charged through the camp, missing one row of sleeping men by a bare eighteen inches. No one was trampled. Terrified more than ever by the sentry's efforts to drive it away, the creature came dashing back through the camp again, this time just missing the tent the captains shared. Scan-

non, Lewis's big Newfoundland, finally drove it out on the prairie by vigorous barking. No damage had been done, except to a few rifles — but it wasn't a restful night.

The trip up the Missouri, arduous from the beginning, grew harder now. Every day the men had to uncoil the cordelles and tow the boats. Often this meant wading up to their armpits in water that was colder as they neared the Rockies, coming as it did from the melting ice and snow. Often they had to stand in the chill stream, holding the boats by the gunwales to keep the waves from swamping the craft. When banks were low

enough so that they could tow from shore they had to struggle through slippery mud, dodging occasional small landslides of earth from adjoining bluffs. When they waded, stones cut and bruised their feet. Often it was too painful to don their moccasins again when they emerged from the water.

Worst of all were the sharp thorns of prickly pears, against which the heaviest leather footwear gave no protection. Lewis tried a double thickness of deerskin, plus soles of dry, tough, thick buffalo hide. Even then thorns pierced through. Sitting by the campfire one evening, Clark extracted seventeen thorns from his feet. The men had to watch the ground so closely for prickly pears they could scarcely manage the cordelle.

Early in June, the boats reached a point where the Missouri divided into two approximately equal streams, near what is now Loma, Montana. Here, one big river came in from the south, another from the north. A little way up its course, this northern river was joined by still a third.

Which was the real Missouri? Sacagawea had no idea. Which one would lead them to the passes through the Rocky Mountains? The Indian girl was as confused as the rest of the party. Three men went up the northern river, three others up the southern. Lewis and Clark themselves, strolling off to the highest land they could find near camp, beheld an amazing stretch of country ahead. Whichever way they looked, they saw vast rolling plains, covered with grazing buffalo, with wolves trailing along the fringes of the herds, waiting to snatch sick animals, or calves that wandered from their mother's protection. Here and there were elk, elsewhere antelope. Far in the distance they could now see snow-capped mountains. But they could not see far enough along the rivers to decide which one to follow.

The reports the men brought back were not very helpful, either. The northern river, they said, was sluggish, with a bed of mud and gravel. Apparently it flowed a long way through the plains. The southern river was clear, flowing swiftly over a bed of rounded stones. That looked as if it came directly from the Rocky Mountains. No one could be sure which stream the expedition should follow. The only possible alternative was to explore still farther.

Next morning each officer led a separate scouting party. Lewis, with six men, went up the northern river; Clark, with five men, went up the southern. Lewis, after traveling sixty miles in three days, knew he was on the wrong stream. He could see now that it led north; the expedition wanted to go west. He came back to the base camp to find that the others had better news. After forty miles of travel along the south fork, Clark had seen snow-capped peaks, both to the north and south. Plainly this stream would lead them to some pass through the mountains.

They were not yet ready to plunge forward, however. Clark needed time to plot the new river courses on his map. Both captains now knew that the southern stream was the real Missouri, but what might they name the large northern fork? Lewis called it Maria's River, in honor of a cousin.

Clark had already named two rivers for girls of his acquaintance, Martha's River and Judith's River. No one knows who Martha was, but Judith's River was named for Judy Hancock, a Kentucky girl of whom young William Clark was growing very fond. Because everyone called her Judy, Clark had always supposed her name was Judith. Not until the expedition returned did he discover she had been christened Julia. But that was of small matter to the girl who soon was Clark's bride. And the river is "Judith's River" on United States maps to this day.

While Clark was busy with topography the other men were ridding themselves of the heavier baggage, which would be almost impossible to carry over the mountains and would not be needed again until the return journey should they not meet the ship. Leaving it at this point would mean one less boat to manage; and badly needed extra hands would be free to row, pole, and pull the remaining boats up the ever swifter and colder stream tumbling down from the mountains.

To STORE their surplus baggage so that it would be safe until their return, the explorers built a *cache* (as French-Canadian woodsmen called these hiding places). Cruzat, who knew the wiliness of the Plains Indians, took charge of its careful construction. First he cut a twenty-inch circle of thick prairie sod, skillfully keeping it in one unbroken piece. Through this opening, a hole was excavated, six or seven feet into the earth, and enlarged in the shape of a great jug underneath the adjoining sod, which was left undisturbed. A protective mattress of sticks was laid on the bottom to keep the expedition's stores safe and dry from any water that might seep in.

Into the cache went the blacksmith's forge and tools, the reserve rations, watertight lead kegs of gunpowder, traps, skins, and scientific specimens. These were covered with hides and over them earth was tightly packed. Above this, the unbroken circle of original sod was fitted back into place. After the grass had grown for a few days, there was not a sign that the earth had ever been disturbed.

All rifles were overhauled and given a final inspection. Private Shields, a clever fellow with his hands, fitted a new spring into Lewis's air gun. Leaks in the canoes were calked. A big pirogue, which they were leaving behind, was pulled from the water up on a small island, and lashed fast to trees, so that floods could not sweep it away. Since, in spite of all the care Cruzat had taken, Indians might still find and loot the big cache, the explorers made several small ones in other places, each containing an extra axe and enough gunpowder for emergencies.

While all this preparation was proceeding, Lewis and Sacagawea had both been taken ill. Lewis, in the medical custom of the day, bled Sacagawea — drawing off a small quantity of

blood; and he dosed himself with medicine. When the party was once again ready to start, Lewis, though still weak, believed himself well enough to move overland. He took with him a few men, including Drouilliard, who would serve as interpreter if they met friendly Indians. Charbonneau remained in one of the boats with Clark to interpret in case they met Indians along the river.

Lewis had not walked any great distance before he began to feel severe pain and a high fever. Though he had no drugs with him, he knew that "medicine" grew almost everywhere, having learned a good deal about healing plants from his mother. He had the men collect small twigs of chokecherry, strip them of leaves, cut them into two-inch lengths, and boil them down to a thick, black brew. Two pints of this, taken one hour apart, a good night's sleep, plus another pint of the bitter black fluid when he arose, and Captain Lewis felt like a new man. By ten o'clock in the morning he was helping to kill two grizzlies!

On the third day of his overland journey, while the others were busy hunting, Lewis pushed ahead with a single companion. Presently he heard the distant sound of falling water and began to see mist rising in the air and drifting away like smoke. The roar of water grew ever louder.

Soon, scrambling up a rocky mass, these two became the first white men ever to behold the Great Falls of the Missouri. They looked down

in awe upon a magnificent spectacle. Even today, when their beauty has been sadly marred by
a power dam, the Great Falls make a striking
picture. But Lewis saw them at their primitive
best, with the wild Missouri's full flood foaming
down over the rocks, throwing up a spray so thick
that the sunlight shining through it made a rain-
bow. Stirred by the beauty of what he saw,
Lewis tried to capture an adequate description in
writing — while the stolid soldier who was his
companion simply began fishing, his thoughts
entirely on his supper.

When Clark arrived with the boats a few days
later, there were new problems. The bleeding
of Sacagawea had not helped her, and such treatment as Clark could give her had brought no
better results. It began to look as if the girl
might die, in which case the expedition would
have a four-month-old baby on its hands and no
way to provide milk. There was nothing they
could do except make the brave squaw comfortable and let her rest, while they faced the next
great problem: how to get their boats around the

Great Falls and the series of dangerous rapids just above. Before they could move the heavy boats and tons of equipment they would have to clear a portage sixteen miles long.

Clark went ahead to mark the best route with stakes and flags, while the men searched for timber to make wheels. In this Montana prairie country, where trees were always scarce, it was hard to get enough wood even for campfires. Eventually, however, they found a cottonwood big enough to serve their purposes. By sawing part of the trunk into slices, they acquired disks of wood, which did not make very good wheels but would at least revolve. With these they managed to make two clumsy wagons. When they found the prairie winds were blowing in the right direction, they took sails from the boats, rigged them on the wagons, and "sailed" over the prairies, though no one has ever discovered just how they managed to steer. Probably the sails were merely used to ease some of the labor of hauling, while men still tugged on the ropes.

In the tremendous heat, the men stripped off

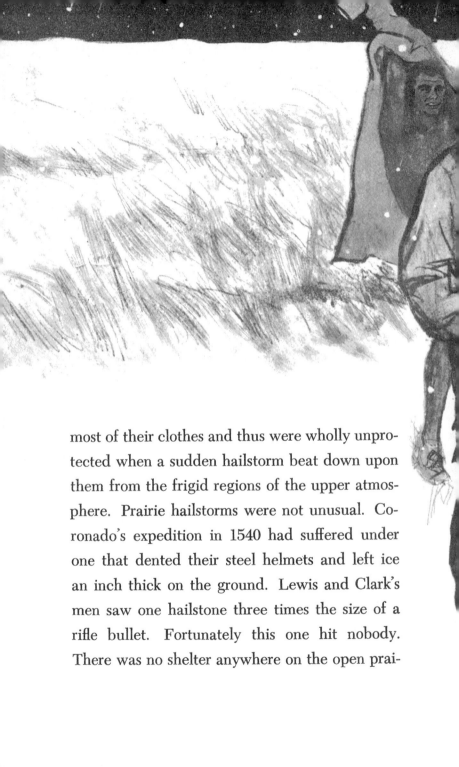

most of their clothes and thus were wholly unprotected when a sudden hailstorm beat down upon them from the frigid regions of the upper atmosphere. Prairie hailstorms were not unusual. Coronado's expedition in 1540 had suffered under one that dented their steel helmets and left ice an inch thick on the ground. Lewis and Clark's men saw one hailstone three times the size of a rifle bullet. Fortunately this one hit nobody. There was no shelter anywhere on the open prai-

rie. One man was knocked to the ground three times during the half hour in which the hail pelted down. Several were bleeding by the time the storm stopped. Lewis took prompt measures to restore morale. Getting out a bottle and gathering some of the ice, he offered everyone a drink of iced punch.

Clark and the Charbonneau family had narrowly escaped death. With Sacagawea, her husband, and the baby, the captain had been busy mapping the river, a task that kept him on low ground not far above the water level. To escape the hail and the sheets of rain, they all sought refuge in a narrow gully, never guessing how swiftly their bone-dry shelter could transform itself into a raging torrent, as the sloping prairies poured water into it. Suddenly, they were in three feet of water, which was swiftly rising around them. As the two men helped Sacagawea up the steep banks with the baby, Charbonneau again completely lost his head. He simply stood as if transfixed, halfway to safety, refusing to budge. The flood reached Clark's waist before he could induce the terrified man to climb. Safe on the high bluffs at last, they looked down into a muddy torrent fifteen feet deep, rushing through their recent refuge.

The faithful York, who had been on the prairie hunting buffalo, returned with no more damage than a drenching.

Lewis met with disappointment when the hard labor of the portage was over and all the rapids had been passed. Now was the time to assemble the framework of his cherished invention, the collapsible boat that the expedition had carried, unassembled, all the way from the distant east.

The iron framework was easily fastened together. But where would they find materials to cover it? Here were no birch or elm trees to strip of their bark. Lewis had not visualized in advance this problem posed by a treeless country.

The explorers had, however, seen the leather boats of the Mandan Indians. So they stitched together buffalo and elk hides and stretched them over the iron frame. Lacking the pine pitch used by eastern Indians to make canoes watertight, they smeared the skins and the seams with a mixture of beeswax, charcoal, and buffalo tallow. After two coats had been applied, the captain was delighted to see that his boat floated "like a perfect cork on the water." But only for a little while! In a few hours, the waterproofing was cracking and scaling, and water was pouring into the boat. There was absolutely no way to make the "Experiment" float. Sadly, Lewis abandoned the project. The men constructed dugout canoes instead, from such trees as they could find.

The two leaders were now giving anxious thought to their failure to find Indians. North America was such a vast empty expanse in those days that the expedition, after leaving the Sioux and Mandans, had traveled hundreds of miles without seeing a single human being. Although occasional "Indian sign" revealed that a few redskins were about, they remained invisible. Once they found bark peeled from trees, which, Sacagawea told them, meant that Indians had been gathering the soft inner layers for food.

At last, on July 20, they saw smoke signals rising far ahead. This meant that Indians had

quietly approached near enough to detect their presence, and had slipped away unseen and were now signaling their tribe. Clark knew it was a favorite device of the redskins to reconnoiter, not always in preparation for attack, but often merely to see the travelers. He therefore left gifts where they could be easily found. These peace offerings were mostly garments and lengths of linen cloth; but Clark also left with these objects, symbolic messages indicating that the travelers were white men and friends. Either Sacagawea or Drouilliard must have helped make the simple little drawings that the Indians could easily understand and interpret. As a further sign of peace, Lewis hoisted flags on the boats. No war party would ever call attention to itself in this way.

Fearful lest the sound of the hunters' rifles might alarm the Indians, Clark personally scouted the countryside for three miles ahead of the boats, before allowing the men to kill game.

Next morning, Clark once again pushed ahead on foot, taking only Charbonneau and one other man with him. All three were very weary by the time they reached another point where the route became doubtful. This was the Three Forks of the Missouri, where the stream splits into three branches of about equal size. Neither Clark nor his men were in any condition to explore farther. Clark himself had chills and fever. Every muscle ached and he could hardly eat. Charbonneau had hurt an ankle. The other man's feet were so sore he could scarcely travel, though he did manage to kill a fawn for their supper.

Charbonneau, clumsy as ever and still unable to swim, chose this dismal moment to fall into the river. Clark, despite his chills, fever, and aching muscles, had to plunge into the icy water to save him. As if this were not enough, two grizzly bears now appeared. The three weary and weakened men had to kill them both before they could settle down safely for the night.

But neither illness nor grizzly bears could stop William Clark. Next morning, after leaving a note for Lewis at the Three Forks, the sick man went up the Middle Fork and then explored the

North Fork briefly. He found Lewis and the boats waiting for him when he returned. All the men were now thoroughly exhausted. The current was so swift that oars were useless. Poles slipped on the flat stones of the river bottom. The resourceful Lewis solved this problem by putting sharp-pointed "gigs," originally intended for spearing fish, on the ends of the poles.

Though it was only July, winter comes so early in the Montana mountains that the officers knew they would have to advance swiftly to cross the Rockies before the early snows began to block the passes. To do this, they must now acquire horses from the Indians — but they still could find no Indians. Clark by this time was too tired for land travel; his feet had been badly bruised by stones and pierced by thorns. The men were all weary. And, most discouraging of all, no one knew which way to go. If by ill chance they chose the wrong route now they would lose so much time the snow would certainly close the passes. In that case, the expedition would be a failure.

When Clark awoke next morning, feeling somewhat stronger, he and Lewis sent a few men along the Southeast Fork, while hunters went out to find meat. The explorers of the Southeast Fork reported that it seemed to lead in the wrong direction. Clark thought the same of the Middle Fork. The only possibility now was to try the North Fork.

There was a little encouragement in the fact that Sacagawea had begun at last to recognize some features of the country in which, she said, her own band of Shoshones had lived. She had been able to describe the Three Forks of the Missouri accurately before the boats reached them. She recognized a creek where, she said, the Shoshones dug white earth to use as paint. Soon she recognized a hill, because it was shaped like a beaver's head. But, even in this country where she had grown up, the Indian girl could not tell the puzzled white men which branch of the river to take, for she had been a mere child when kidnaped.

Before they set off up the North Fork, Lewis

and Clark paused to name the rivers. The Southeast Fork they called Gallatin's River, after Albert Gallatin, Secretary of the Treasury — who was paying for the expedition. The Middle Fork they called Madison's River, for James Madison, Secretary of State, whose diplomacy had helped make the expedition possible. The North Fork became Jefferson's River, in honor of "the author of our enterprise." It is amusing to note that both young men named the rivers they first discovered for girls they knew. Only later, when the girls had been duly honored, did they begin naming rivers farther west for eminent statesmen.

Still watching hopefully for Shoshone Indians, they pushed on. The Shoshones were a rather forlorn mountain tribe living on the eastern foothills of the Rockies. Because they dwelt so far from the white men they could get almost no firearms and still had to depend on bows and arrows. Only in their remote uplands, where food was hard to get, could the Shoshones feel safe from the better-armed Plains Indians. When they ventured down to the buffalo plains to hunt, they were in constant danger from the merciless and well-armed Blackfeet and Minnetarees, who lived far enough to the east to obtain arms and ammunition from white traders.

Signs that Indians were about began to multiply. Far off on the plains, pillars of smoke began to rise again, signals to other red hunters to move back to safety in the mountains. Although the white men had yet to see an Indian, the Indians had once again seen them. Clark found footprints. Following the trail, he found it led to a little hill, from which some Indian scout had been secretly watching the camp. Sacagawea was sure her own tribe was somewhere near.

Since Clark, with a large and painful carbuncle forming on his ankle, could no longer walk, Lewis took his turn leading the party along the shore. Determined to find Indians somehow, he struck off into the plains on August 1, 1805. It was a journey almost as discouraging as Clark's, for Drouilliard was the only healthy man in the group. Lewis himself, though not so ill as Clark, was recovering from dysentery. Sergeant Gass had a lame back, Charbonneau a game leg. But in spite of all handicaps, they covered forty-five miles in two days, until Gass and Charbonneau could go no farther. Lewis tried to press on with Drouilliard, who immediately had a fall so serious that for a short time he could not even rise from the ground.

With the whole party incapacitated, there was nothing to do but camp and await the boats, which were now having great difficulty pushing upstream against the swift current. Sometimes the wading men could hold themselves upright only by clutching bushes along the bank. Several had developed painful boils — apparently a product of their fatigue. Their feet were bruised by struggling over stones in the many rapids, which increased in number as they drew nearer the mountains.

When Lewis was once again able to travel, he walked upstream to yet another fork. Here he met with a mishap unique in the history of exploration. He left a note for Clark telling him which stream to ascend. The note was fastened to a small pole along the riverbank. There was nothing unusual about this. The explorers often left such messages. But Lewis made the mistake of cutting his pole from fresh, green wood. After he had gone on, a beaver wandered by, nibbled at the fresh bark on the pole, and upset it, so that the note blew away. Clark, arriving with the boats and finding nothing to guide him, went up the wrong stream. By pure luck Drouilliard, hunting between the two valleys, stumbled upon Clark and brought him back to the right tributary.

Misfortunes began to multiply as the stream grew steeper, swifter, colder, and more difficult. One man barely escaped with his life when he fell in front of a boat, which ran over him. A few inches of water between his body and the heavy keel saved him from being crushed against the stony river bottom, and he managed to emerge before being drowned.

Suddenly, game animals virtually disappeared and food grew scarce. There were no more Indian signs. Private George Shannon now got lost again. Although signal shots and blasts on the bugle did not bring him in and two searches failed, he eventually turned up, three days later. This time he was well fed, having taken along enough ammunition to kill three deer.

These difficulties the expedition could surmount, but the failure to find Indians might soon prove disastrous. Lewis would have to forge ahead of the boats, once again looking for Shoshones. Leaving special written instructions as to what he wanted done in case he was killed, the captain started off on August 9, 1805, taking Drouilliard and two other men. He left behind the regretful Clark, who would have liked to go along but could now scarcely move because of his infection and weakness.

Next day, near what is today Grayling, Montana, Lewis found an Indian trail leading toward the mountains. Following it upstream to another fork, he again left a note, asking Clark to camp there and wait for him. This time, he was careful to leave his message on a "dry willow pole," without any green bark that might tempt wandering beavers.

As he pushed up the new tributary (now known as Prairie Creek), the Indian trail grew steadily fainter, but there were the marks of horses' hoofs. The Indians could not be very far away — and obviously had horses. Presently, the trail vanished entirely, but a pass through the hills ahead became visible. Lewis sent Drouilliard back to leave a second note, giving Clark new instructions which way to come. Meanwhile Lewis himself pushed on, hoping now to find Indians at almost any moment.

WHEN DROUILLIARD returned, Lewis outlined his tactics. Shields was sent to one far flank and Drouilliard to the other. Lewis with a single soldier maintained the center of this advancing line. The first man to discover any trace of another Indian trail was to put his hat on his rifle and raise it silently. It was too dangerous to signal in any other way. A shot or even a shout might alarm the Indians, who presumably were in the immediate vicinity.

For about a mile the line moved forward, discovering nothing of interest. Then about two miles ahead Lewis saw something moving. Snatching his telescope he looked again. He could now plainly make out a mounted redskin riding toward the white men, obviously unaware of their presence. The warrior's costume was un-like any Lewis had previously seen. That meant he belonged to a new tribe, who could only be the Shoshones — and he had a horse.

The problem now was to advance within speaking distance without frightening the Shoshone away. If they could get close enough, Drouilliard would be able to make himself understood through the sign language. When Sacagawea arrived with the boats, interpretation would be easy.

At the distance of about a mile the warrior, seeing the white men at last, halted to watch them. Swiftly pulling a blanket from his pack, Lewis waved it over his head, then spread it on the ground, as if in preparation for a guest. It was the usual gesture of friendship in sign language.

Though Lewis made this friendly sign three times, the Indian remained immovable, watching suspiciously. Just then Drouilliard and Shields, who had been struggling through under-brush, came into sight on the open plain. To the lone red warrior, it appeared that one white was

attempting to rivet his attention, while the others
slipped in behind him.

Snatching up some beads, a looking glass, and
other trinkets, Lewis walked slowly forward.
The Indian let him approach to within 200 yards
before he turned his horse and began to ride
away. Almost in despair, Lewis shouted after him
the only Shoshone word he knew.

"Tab-ba-bo-ne!" he yelled.

Lewis was trying to say "white man," but Sacagawea's lessons in the Shoshone language had not been very successful. The word was really *tai-va-vo-ne*. At least that is the way Shoshones pronounce it in our day. It does not really mean "white man" but "stranger." Sacagawea had done the best she could. However, it is probable that in their remote mountain home the Shoshones saw so few white men that they had no specific name for them. Sacagawea had thus selected the most appropriate word she could think of. In the foothills of the Rockies in those days, a white man was certainly a "stranger." By the same token, any stranger in that wild country was likely to be an enemy. Seeing three unknown men approaching, one of them shouting that he was a stranger, the Shoshone naturally remained very suspicious.

To quiet the Indian's fears, Lewis signaled his men to halt. Drouilliard obeyed. Shields, failing to understand, went stupidly plodding ahead. Watching Shields the Indian let Lewis come fifty paces nearer, still holding up the presents and repeating the word *tab-ba-bo-ne* and pulling up his sleeves to show the white skin of his upper arms (for by this time the exposed hands and faces of the whole exploring party were bronzed to the color of the Indians).

The lone warrior let Lewis approach still nearer before he whirled, lashed his horse with his whip, and disappeared into the willow underbrush. It was a heartbreaking moment. After their long desperate search they had found an Indian whose tribe possessed horses, only to frighten him into flight.

All that the white men could do was to follow the trail of the vanished redskin, which after three miles turned up into the hills. The warrior would certainly warn the rest of the Indian camp, wherever it was. The only procedure the white men could follow was to act as unlike a hostile war party as possible. Picking a conspicuous spot that could be seen from all directions, they built a fire and began cooking a meal. It was a virtual guaranty of peaceful intentions. But it produced no desirable results.

When no more Shoshones appeared, Lewis,

after hanging gifts on a pole near the ashes, took up the trail again. He re-emphasized his friendliness by carrying an American flag, plainly visible for miles. No Shoshone would know what it was, but it would show plainly that the strangers were not trying to conceal themselves, as would hostile Indians.

Though they saw no more Shoshones, they were delighted to find the tracks of eight or ten horses; and it was encouraging to find that the next stream was flowing west. They knew they had not yet reached the highest point in North America, for they could now see the Rockies towering ahead of them; but, since the water ran toward the sunset, they had crossed the Great Continental Divide. If the stream could pass through the Rockies, so could they — if they found horses.

Suddenly, on August 13, they saw more Indians — two squaws and a warrior, this time — who fled, paying no heed to Lewis's renewed shouts of "Tab-ba-bo-ne." Once again, all that the explorers could do was to follow the trail. As they were toiling silently through a series of small twisting ravines they came upon an old squaw, a young one, and a little girl. Neither group saw the other until they were close at hand. The young squaw disappeared, running swiftly. The old one, knowing she had no chance to escape, sat down with the child, as Indians sometimes did, to wait quietly for death. As Lewis walked up to them, a stranger and therefore an enemy, both submissively lowered their heads for the toma-hawk.

The Lewis and Clark expedition had found Shoshones at last. All it had to do now was to make friends with them. Lewis took the old

woman gently by the hand, repeating the word
tab-ba-bo-ne and again pulling up his sleeve to
show that he was white. The old squaw had
probably never seen a white man, but she could
see this was not a raiding warrior of a hostile
tribe. Lewis continued to repeat that he was
"a stranger." She could see that for herself,
though it was not quite what Lewis was intend-
ing to say. This unknown man could scarcely be
an enemy, since obviously he had no desire to kill
her. His face was not painted for war; was, in
fact, not painted at all! He was giving her presents — beads, moccasins, awls, mirrors, paint!

When Drouilliard joined them, Lewis instructed him to request the old squaw to call back
the young squaw who had run away. She must
have been hiding somewhere near, for she soon
reappeared and was delighted to receive a gift of
several trinkets. All faces now were painted with
vermilion, which Lewis knew — probably
through Sacagawea — was a Shoshone symbol of
peace. In sign language Drouilliard asked the
women to take them to the Shoshone camp.

They had gone but two miles when they met sixty Shoshone warriors, armed exclusively with bows and arrows save for three Indians with fire-arms. This war party was on its way to drive off what they supposed to be a Minnetaree attack. Dropping his rifle but carrying the flag, Lewis advanced alone with his three men, the squaws, and the child following fifty paces behind him. The Shoshones could see this was no enemy, especially when they found the squaws unhurt and proudly displaying all their gifts. At once they embraced their embarrassed visitors, each warrior throwing his left arm over each white man's shoulders and pressing his greasy, painted cheek against the white man's. Lewis remarks in his journal that they were "besmeared with their grease and paint till I was heartily tired of the national hug."

When Lewis offered the pipe of peace, all the warriors sat in a circle to council on the spot, pulling off their moccasins as they did so, an act symbolic of good faith and sincerity. It expressed their willingness to go barefoot for ever, should

they prove treacherous ("a pretty heavy penalty if they are to march through the plains of their country," noted Lewis in his journal, remembering his own sufferings from stones and prickly pears).

First they had smoked, a solemn ritual which was part of every council. Then Lewis explained, with Drouilliard interpreting in sign language, that he came as a friend of the Shoshones. Later at the Shoshone camp he would reveal who the white men were, whence they came, and whither they were going. Meantime, it was very hot; the white men had no water; they were tired and thirsty and would like to visit the Shoshones in their village. The chief, Ca-me-âh-wait, made a friendly speech and received the American flag from Lewis. Then they started for camp together.

There was another council as soon as they arrived. This time they smoked the tribe's own special ceremonial peace pipe, made of semitransparent stone, hollowed out and polished by some ancient, primitive craftsman. Like many Indian pipes, it did not have the usual upturned bowl but was a cylinder, with its bowl pointing forward much like a modern cigarette holder.

It was disappointing to find that the Shoshones had no meat, had, in fact, nothing to eat except cakes made of dried berries; but that made it easy for the visitors to prove their friendship. In a short time Drouilliard shot three deer. The Shoshones were so hungry they devoured even the entrails and the soft parts of the hoofs.

After some persuasion, a portion of the tribe agreed to take pack horses down to the forks of the stream to meet Clark. They seemed to become more and more nervous as they descended from the shelter of their hills. One Indian after another began to slip away back to the mountains, until only a handful remained. It was an anxious moment. If these few remaining redskins grew distrustful, they too would disappear, and their horses would disappear with them.

When Lewis and the Shoshones reached the forks, Clark had not yet arrived, and the letters that had been left for him were still there. Strange to say, this helped to impress the Indians. The red men did not quite know what these queer white objects with black marks upon them might signify, but they looked like powerful medicine of some kind. Drouilliard went downstream with another letter, which urged Clark to hurry. Anxiously, Lewis waited, for he knew the Shoshones might at any moment grow tired of waiting and disappear into the hills.

Two hours later the problem solved itself. An excited Shoshone came rushing upstream with news that he had seen more white men and their boats. It was a joyful moment for Lewis, save for the fact that the delighted Shoshones insisted on embracing him all over again, till he was daubed once more with paint and grease. A few Indians started downstream with horses.

While all this had been happening, Clark had had no idea where Lewis was or how he had fared. Suddenly he saw Sacagawea begin to dance joyfully as she pointed to mounted Indians approaching. As she danced, she sucked her fingertips. It was sign language: "My own people, among whom I was nursed." A little while later

Clark, Sacagawea, and Charbonneau rode up to the forks, where Lewis was waiting for them. As Sacagawea appeared, a squaw rushed to embrace her. Lewis had not only found Shoshones. He had found the very band from which Sacagawea had been kidnaped.

At the Shoshone camp there was a third council. Usually these serious gatherings were for chiefs and warriors only. This one was attended by Sacagawea, who replaced with real Shoshone speech Drouilliard's sign language. Suddenly, seeing for the first time Chief Ca-me-âh-wait, the young squaw leaped up, ran to him, threw her blanket around him, embraced him, and burst into tears. She had recognized her brother. Even this chief, though by tradition of iron composure, showed a few signs of emotion. As yet he was careful not to let her know that in the years since she had been captured most of the family had died.

The exploring party proposed in their turn to receive the Indian leaders in council at the forks. On a level stretch of grass the men set up a canopy made with a canvas sail and willow boughs, under which the red men and the white met in what was really a business conference. The Indians wanted white men's goods, especially firearms. The white men wanted horses. The explorers could not part with their rifles, for by this time they needed all they had left; but the captains explained that if the Shoshones would only aid the expedition with their horses white traders in the not too distant future would bring firearms, ammunition, and other goods all the way to the Shoshone country.

Ca-me-âh-wait explained that though his band did not have as many horses as the expedition would need, he himself would go west through the Lemhi Pass and procure more animals from the other Shoshone bands. Lewis and Clark were, however, able to buy three horses on the spot, and the chief received a U.S. Army uniform coat, a shirt, scarlet leggings, tobacco, and a Jefferson peace medal. Subordinate chiefs received old medals with George Washington's picture. There was a feast, and the Shoshones were shown York, Scannon the Newfoundland, and the air gun.

Packsaddles were fashioned at the forks, horses at last obtained, and another secret cache built for supplies that would be needed on the return journey the following year. Since the canoes could not be hidden, the explorers simply filled them with stones and sank them in the river. The stones would hold them firmly against floods and they would be safe from possible fires.

As a final gesture of friendship, the white men held one more council and made a great feast, at which they offered the Shoshones some of the dried squash they had carried all the way from the Mandan village. The finest food he had ever tasted, said Ca-me-âh-wait politely. Some of the men also made what they called a "bush drag," a crude fishing net made of flexible willow twigs, woven together, with which they caught more than 500 fish, most of which they gave to their Shoshone friends, who had neither fishhooks nor nets and could catch fish only with bone-pointed spears.

With nine horses and a mule purchased outright, plus two rented horses, the expedition began to move its baggage from the river to the Indian camp. The squaws, who were used to heavy labor, carried all that the horses could not manage. In the village a few days later Lewis and Clark were able to buy more horses. They also hired a Shoshone guide, promptly nicknamed "Old Toby."

Four of his sons and one other Indian accompanied Toby and the white men as they took the pack train down the Lemhi River and across the Bitterroot Mountains. Although they had left the Shoshone village on August 30, 1805, they soon found they had begun their journey not a day too soon. As they went farther into the mountains, snow and sleet began to strike them, and by September 4 everything was frozen. They narrowly avoided a battle with some Selish Indians, who prepared for conflict the moment they saw York. Black paint to them was war paint. Everything was peaceable again when they discovered York's natural color, although again he had to submit to the usual tests with the wet fingertips of skeptical redskins. Other Selish, coming into camp, had welcome news. There was an "old white man" only "five sleeps" ahead. Though the expedition never found this imaginary character, the report showed that other white men had been visiting the country just beyond. A few days later, when the explorers met the first of the Nez Percé tribe, there was additional news of white men ahead.

It was a desperately difficult struggle over the high Lolo Trail, which to this day is wild terrain. The men were almost exhausted as they neared the other side of the mountains. The cold grew more intense. Storm-toppled trees, crashing around them, increased the danger. With only moccasins for protection, their feet were nearly frozen. Their only water was melted snow. Twice Lewis's horse went astray with all his personal baggage. Other horses lost their footing and rolled down the steep slopes. Food gave out. Hunters could find no meat except two wild horses and a colt. They dared not eat their own pack horses, or they would never have been able to move their baggage. They ate candles, a wolf, and crayfish, almost anything that could sustain life.

Then as they came down the western slopes into warmer air they discovered new troubles. It was warm enough for wasps and hornets — so many that the torture of their stings drove the horses frantic.

Clark pressed ahead, and presently Lewis's men found along the trail Clark's encouraging note saying that food would soon be plentiful. Later one of the men came in with a bag of salmon and some Indian bread made of roots. Their days of starvation were over. That evening

Clark himself rejoined the party, with news that he had met friendly Nez Percé Indians and had found a large branch of the Columbia River. Hunters brought in four deer and two more salmon. There was much to be thankful for.

CLARK REPORTED that he had found his way to the Clearwater, a large tributary of the mighty Columbia. His good news came not a moment too soon, for Lewis and the men of his rear contingent were so battered and weary from their long struggle across the Rockies that many were unable to walk the few remaining miles to the comfortable rest camp Clark had established. These exhausted men had to be placed on pack horses. Lewis himself was barely able to hold himself in the saddle. Almost everyone was ill. Only good food, rest, and medical attention could restore the Corps of Discovery to an effective exploration party once again.

At this moment, when the explorers were as nearly helpless as they ever were on the entire trip to the Pacific, they barely escaped an Indian massacre. They were completely unaware of their peril, and it was not until decades later that the Nez Percés let slip the tale of what might well have meant the total destruction of the expedition.

. The Indian story, handed down from father to son for generations, reveals that as these strangers approached the Indians made plans to kill them to the last man. By good fortune, however, a squaw named Wat-ku-ese (Stray Away), whose life had once been saved by two white trappers, pleaded against the massacre. "Do not be afraid of them," she said gently, insisting that they held no animosity for their red brothers.

Her tribe heeded her words and upon meeting the white men found them very friendly. In fact the Nez Percés remained on excellent terms with all white explorers and settlers for the next seventy years.

Never even guessing the narrowness of their escape, Lewis and Clark held the usual council. Three chiefs received medals. The white men so impressed the Nez Percés with their dancing that the legend lingered on into the present century.

When the explorers recovered their strength, all set to work cutting trees and hollowing logs to fashion dugout canoes. The Nez Percés offered to care for the horses till the white men returned up the river. When the little fleet of canoes pushed off down the Clearwater on the last lap of their westward journey, Nez Percé chiefs accompanied them for some miles.

This appeared to be the easiest part of the route, since it was all downstream. But although it was almost effortless to float down the swift western rivers, it was continuously dangerous. On the second day a canoe struck a rock, then swung against another, split, and soon filled with water.

All the men climbed safely to the rocks, where those who could not swim clung perilously, surrounded by the roaring water, until rescuers could reach them.

A few days later, three more canoes smashed into rocks. The men in one canoe were marooned on a stony perch in the rising river for an hour before they could be brought to safety. Other canoemen, farther downstream, fished from the water any equipment that floated. An Indian, swimming as easily as an otter, went out to save more of the baggage. The lead canisters of gunpowder lashed securely to the log canoes were safe, but tomahawks and shot pouches sank in the torrent.

Though wild game was scarce, food was no longer a serious problem — if you liked to eat dogs. These could be purchased in any Indian village along the river. As we have seen, Lewis thought dog meat "an agreeable food," or at any rate more to his taste than horse, lean venison, or lean elk. He was convinced that the men were healthier on a daily diet of three square meals of dog than they had ever been since passing beyond the buffalo country. Clark, though he admitted dog was a nourishing diet, never confused it with breast of chicken. The men soon learned to tolerate it, some even preferring dog meat to fresh-caught salmon.

The Columbia River Indians were friendly, partly because they were aware of the white traders who visited the lower reaches of the Columbia, and partly because they could see a woman with a baby in the approaching canoes. The Indians usually realized that this did not constitute a war party (although a few communities took fright and fled at sight of the floating expedition).

Signs of the white man's influence on the region became more frequent as they descended the river. A few Indians were wearing red or blue cloth jackets. Others had brass kettles, cloth trousers, shirts, pistols, beads, and metal powder flasks. Soon they were meeting Indians who knew a few words of English.

The expedition passed two danger points in safety. One was at the Short Narrows, where the entire current of the mighty Columbia River rushes between rocky walls less than forty-five yards apart, "swelling, boiling and whorling in every direction." The expedition's expert riverman, Cruzat, brought the canoes safely down

through this swift water. A single miscalculation would have meant instant death. Cruzat's skill saved the labor and delay that a portage would have required. But when the explorers reached the Cascades, where the Columbia drops sixty feet in two miles, not even Cruzat dared risk the roaring river. The men, working like pack animals, carried boats and baggage over a toilsome portage skirting the jagged rocks and foaming white water.

By early November, the discoverers were floating easily down the lower reaches of the broad Columbia, looking in wonder at the immense trees of the Oregon forests. These were not so gigantic as the "big trees" of the California coast, which Lewis and Clark's men never saw; but to Eastern eyes they were big enough. Some towered two hundred feet toward the sky, were ten or fifteen feet in diameter at the base as surviving stumps in Oregon still testify. Here and there along the shore, leaping from stone cliffs against a background of the green forest, exquisite cascades of falling water poured down in a froth of white foam — through nothing but thin air.

Beautiful though this Columbia River country was, the explorers were wretchedly miserable for a time. The sheer walls of rock came so near the shore that the men could find no dry or level land to camp upon. Dry firewood was hard to find, and often the men were cold. One night they attempted to sleep on driftwood massed in the water along the shore. It was not a comfortable night. They had dined on a few dried fish purchased from the Indians; and all night long the driftwood stirred restlessly on the uneasy bosom of the river.

But all their discomforts seemed of no importance when on a momentous day Clark could write in his journal: "Ocian in view! O! the joy." There is some doubt whether the explorers really did see the ocean that day. They may have seen merely the wide estuary of the lower Columbia. But it meant the same thing. They had won their way across the Continent.

They had reached the mighty Pacific that they had been "so long anxious to see" and they delighted in the roar of the waves breaking on the rocky shore. Not even the conquistador Balboa could have felt deeper emotions.

Thomas Jefferson's dream had come true; his

brave captains and their Corps of Discovery had fought their way up the Missouri, over the unknown and terrible Rockies, and down the Columbia, mapping the route every mile of the way. The continent could be crossed. Lewis and Clark had just done it. And where explorers map a route, traders and settlers follow.

True, the brig *Lydia* of Boston twice missed connections with the expedition, and thus deprived them of an easy passage home. But the unworried explorers were soon busy building a fort and winter camp from the excellent timber available, making salt from sea water, and exploring the surrounding countryside.

By Christmas 1805 every member of the party was snugly settled in new cabins, well heated by big fireplaces, with fortifications surrounding the camp strong enough to deter any Indians tempted to attack.

The winter of 1805–1806 on the far Pacific Coast was safe and comfortable but a little dull. And during that quiet and peaceful season the Corps of Discovery enjoyed a well-earned rest.

W HEN SPRING CAME and still no trading vessels
had appeared, the captains began to make plans
to go home the way they had come. It would
not be so hard a journey as their westward struggle, for they now knew the route and had supplies cached at several points east of the Rockies.
Besides, from the eastern side of the mountains
to St. Louis they would be going downstream,
with the swift Missouri current helping them and
making it possible at times to cover eighty miles
a day.

Though the return trip would be easier than
the journey outward bound, Lewis and Clark
knew it was still possible that hostile Indians
might wipe out the whole expedition. To assure
some record of what they had done, they wrote a

short account of their long journey, to which they added a map and a list of the men involved. They left several copies of this behind them.

By the same strange irony as before, Captain Samuel Hill and his brig *Lydia* came sailing back into the Columbia River for the third time, just after Lewis and Clark had left in March, 1806. One copy of the expedition's report fell into Captain Hill's hands. He took it with him by way of China. But when the *Lydia* at last reached Boston in 1807, the whole world already knew what Lewis and Clark had done.

The return trip up the Columbia presented several difficulties. Not long before starting, the expedition lost one of its canoes. An Indian dog had gnawed through the leather mooring rope and let it drift away. There was no time to make another, and the local Indians did not want to sell their precious craft. A canoe among these coastal tribes brought the same price as a new wife. Captain Lewis finally exchanged his gold-laced uniform coat and some of the scanty store of tobacco for one of the Indians' treasured boats.

Although the ammunition was still adequate, food was hard to obtain. The hunters did not always make a kill. Nor were Indians always willing to sell food, especially in view of the fact that the expedition's store of trading goods was nearly exhausted by this time.

Clark procured food one day by "magic." When the Indians refused to sell him supplies, he slyly dropped into their campfire an inch of "port fire match" — a paper case filled with slow-burning powder used by the artillery at that time. The campfire flashed into many-colored flame, terrifying the redskins, who begged this dangerous medicine man to "take out the bad fire." As Clark knew exactly how long an inch of port fire match would burn, his magic extinguished the flame at exactly the proper moment. He was instantly given food!

As they struggled upriver, the explorers again needed horses, until they could reach their own, which they had left with the Nez Percés. They had difficulty securing these pack animals until they discovered that the Indians were greatly impressed by the two officers' skill as physicians. Then they began to get both horses and food supplies in exchange for medical treatment. Lewis and Clark treated rheumatism, applied healing medicine to sore eyes, set a broken arm in splints, lanced abscesses, and even treated a case of paralysis (with at least temporary success). Clark occasionally had fifty patients at a time. He accepted dogs, or rarely a horse, in payment of his fee.

But the few pack animals they had been able to buy coming up the Columbia and Clearwater were not nearly enough to get them across the mountains. And then to add to their troubles they discovered that the Nez Percés had distributed the Lewis and Clark horses among various scattered bands during the winter months. It took precious time to reassemble their mounts, but in the end the expedition started eastward along the Lolo Trail with a pack train of sixty animals.

On June 10, 1806, they were on the move and by the 15th, began what they hoped would be their final push up the western slopes. They had not heeded the Indians' warning that in the mountains there would be no forage for the horses until July. Soon the column reached snow eight to ten feet deep, but packed down so firmly that it took the weight of the horses easily. In a short time, however, everyone began to have doubts about the trail; and when the veteran woodsman Drouilliard thought that even he might lose his way, the captains decided to turn back to attempt to obtain Nez Percé guides.

Temporarily storing most of the baggage, food, instruments, and the precious journals (with their record of two years' adventures), the whole group retraced its steps toward the Nez Percé country. The trail became so nearly impassable that they lost four horses and a mule. One man cut a vein by accident and almost bled to death. When John Colter's horse fell into a stream, both man and steed were swept away, although Colter clung courageously on to his precious rifle until he could scramble out. Food ran so short that for a while they had nothing to eat but mushrooms. which Americans of that era never touched. Then the hunters began to bring in meat again, and the explorers were able to spear a few salmon with their bayonets.

When they reached Nez Percé country once again, Lewis and Clark managed to persuade three warriors to guide them, and soon they met two more helpful tribesmen in the mountains. With the aid of these five Indians they were able by June 26 to reach the place where they had left their baggage. That night a sixth Nez Percé overtook them. Within two days they were over the Great Divide and far enough down the Rockies' eastern slopes to find grass for their hungry horses. Next day they were completely out of the snow.

Their food had been reduced to a few roots; but as the weary horses plodded into the new camp, their riders saw a cheering sight. Hunters who had preceded them displayed with pride a freshly dressed deer ready to roast! Equally welcome after their frigid mountain journey was the fact that the air about the camp was warmed by a hot spring.

The Indians dammed the stream of warm water that ran from it, and everyone bathed luxuriously in the little pool. Lewis soaked for nineteen blissful minutes, Clark for only ten. It was the first hot bath any of them had had in two long years!

The discovers now separated into two distinct parties, so that they could explore as wide a stretch of unknown country as possible.

Lewis would travel overland, north of the Missouri and along Maria's River. This was dangerous country, where it was likely that he would meet the warlike Blackfeet and Prairie Minnetarees (very different from the friendly Minnetarees they had met along the Missouri the year before). Clark would proceed to Jefferson's River, where they had left the canoes. One sergeant and a few men would then take the canoes downstream, while Clark went on to the Yellowstone River and traveled along that still unexplored stream. All three parties would meet again — or so they hoped — somewhere along the main stream of the Missouri.

The whole expedition rested for two days to recover strength. Hunters brought in twelve deer. There was "a plenty of meat and that very good," Clark noted in his journal. Rifles were repaired. Scouts, moving about outside the camp, found the marks of bare human feet and the hoof marks of several horses. It was plain that Indians had been lurking nearby. "Minnetarees," said their frightened Nez Percé guides.

The groups parted company on July 3, 1806, and were not reunited until August 13. During that month and ten days there was enough excitement and danger to keep all the participants constantly on their guard. When Lewis and Clark finally did make contact in August they had interesting tales to tell. Lewis had narrowly missed being cut off by a party of Minnetarees, but had proceeded without serious incident through lush buffalo and grizzly bear country to the Great Falls of the Missouri, thence overland to the Maria's River valley, where food was scarce. In his scuffle with Indians, two redskins were killed and Lewis was very nearly killed himself. Lewis and his small party joined Sergeant Gass where Maria's River enters the Missouri and proceeded down the Missouri seeking Clark.

Clark meanwhile had gone overland to the Yellowstone with a train of forty-nine horses. Sacagawea was again useful as a guide, pointing out an excellent pass through the mountains which brought Clark to the Yellowstone Valley. Though Clark and his men saw only one Indian, the redskins were all about them and contrived to steal all their animals. The party had to make dugouts of trees cut down along the river and other boats of buffalo skins, and float on down the Yellowstone and the Missouri in search of the rest of the expedition.

For a time neither section of the exploration party had the faintest idea where the other section was. During this time Lewis had been accidentally wounded by one of his own men and was in great pain, if not in real danger. The two groups found each other at last, and taking with them the Mandan chief, She-he-ke, his wife Yellow Corn, and their son, began the last and easiest stage of the whole trip down the broad river toward St. Louis.

As THE EXPEDITION'S BOATS swung out into the swift Missouri current, leaving the Mandan village for the last time, Lewis and Clark could not know that the whole United States had given them up for dead. There had been no news concerning them since Corporal Warfington and Pierre Dorion had returned in 1805, except for a vague rumor from some Osage chiefs that Lewis and Clark had crossed the Rockies. This seemed a very unreliable report, particularly since it had been passed from tribe to tribe across the entire expanse of the western prairies.

Untroubled by gloomy thoughts of any kind, the explorers settled exultantly into their boats for the final stage of their tremendous journey. They had achieved their goal. They had crossed the continent, returned with a written record, assembled Indian vocabularies, collected scientific specimens, and opened the way for the expansion of the United States of America into its vast new western territories. They had been forced to fight Indians only once, and even in this instance without losing a single member of the expedition. Not one of the exploring party had been killed. Lewis had been wounded, it is true, but accidentally and by one of his own men. Nothing could have saved poor Sergeant Floyd, the only man who died on the whole journey of discovery.

There was little danger between the Mandan village and St. Louis; and these returning heroes were glad now to have the assistance of the swift current, against which they had struggled so painfully on the outward journey. Aided by oars and sail, they swept downstream at eighty miles a day. On September 22, 1806, the voyagers turned the bows of their boats shoreward at Fort Belle-fontaine, over those palisades the flag with its seventeen proud stars fluttered in the breeze, while the big guns boomed their salute. Next day they landed in St. Louis. Orders were sent across the Mississippi to hold the outgoing United States mails. The horsemen carrying the eastern post must await a special message for the President of the United States, the news that Jefferson had so long desired. Lewis and Clark had accomplished their great mission.

In St. Louis the officers as swiftly as possible wrote preliminary reports, paid off the men, and gave each of them papers entitling them to special grants of land for their services on the expedition. Despite this needful delay, both captains were at the Clark home near Louisville on November 5, 1806. Clark remained with his parents and relatives, while Lewis took the Mandan chief, She-he-ke, to Albemarle County and thence to Washington to visit President Jefferson.

Congress gave the two captains land grants of 1600 acres, while each of the men received 320 acres. President Jefferson then sent Meriwether Lewis back to St. Louis to become governor of Missouri. Clark was promoted to the rank of

Brigadier General commanding the Missouri Militia. Once again the friends were together.

Safely home from all his dangers, famous throughout the nation, enriched by generous land grants, Clark promptly married.

Many years previously when young William Clark had been living at home with his parents, he had been riding one day along a back road in Virginia when he had come suddenly upon two little girls, both on one difficult horse. The nag was obstinate as a mule, and refused to move. Like many horses, this animal understood perfectly that it could safely refuse to obey children. Clark dismounted and led the stubborn creature for a little distance. When he mounted once again, he compelled this balky beast to follow.

The girls were Julia Hancock, usually called "Judy," and Harriet Kennerly, first cousins who had been brought up as sisters. Though they were still no more than children, William Clark fell promptly in love with Julia, and made a firm decision that he would marry her when she was old enough. What neither he nor the girls could possibly know was that eventually he would marry both of them! He became engaged to Julia not long after the expedition returned, married her early in 1808, and took her with him when he returned to St. Louis.

Unlike Clark, Lewis fell vaguely in and out of love with several girls, but apparently he was not the marrying kind. He was handsome, blond, intelligent, but moody, solitary, more in love with nature and the wilderness than with any girl. Even the names of most of his temporary sweethearts are unrecorded (although one, Milly Maury, daughter of his schoolmaster, asked to see his picture once again, as she lay dying long years afterward).

Governor Meriwether Lewis was unhappy during his next two years. He was a soldier, frontiersman, explorer — not the man to deal with the jealousy, greed, and corruption of political life. In spite of the help and loyal friendship of Clark, now married to Julia Hancock, Lewis was constantly plagued by political friction and disputes. It was a life for which he was never fitted and one he did not really understand. After his friend Mr. Jefferson had left the White House, difficulty with the government offices in Washington compounded Lewis's woes in Missouri. Seeing that it would be impossible to straighten out his Washington troubles by correspondence, Governor Lewis gathered together the papers and accounts he needed and set out for the capital on September 4, 1809, first going down the Mississippi to Chickasaw Bluffs (Memphis, Tennessee) and then starting overland through that state. On October 10, 1809, he paused at a frontier farm in Tennessee, called Grinder's Stand, near modern Hohenwald, and asked the settler's wife to let him occupy a cabin for the night. Lewis was suffering from a touch of fever and his behavior during this journey had, at times, seemed odd. Mrs. Grinder noticed that he talked to himself while awaiting his supper, but that is a common habit of people who have lived much alone in the woods.

No one has ever been able to decipher exactly what happened on that tragic night in the lonely clearing at Grinder's Stand. In her own cabin, during the night, Mrs. Grinder heard a shot, perhaps two shots, from the general direction of Lewis's cabin. No two accounts agree. Peering from her own shelter, through cracks between the logs, she saw Lewis, apparently wounded, staggering toward her cabin. He was begging for water. She insisted that she was too frightened to unbar the door.

Was it suicide or murder? Some accounts say that Lewis's body showed he had been shot from behind. That would have been murder. Others say he had slashed himself with a razor. That would indicate suicide. However, his pocketbook had disappeared, which would seem to indicate robbery and violence.

Clark, when he first received the news, remembered Lewis's many personal worries and anxieties. He wrote his brother, Jonathan Clark: "I fear O! I fear the weight of his mind has overcome him." But in later years Clark always denied that Lewis could possibly have been a suicide.

The old friendship, the long and affectionate association, was broken at last. These lives so closely united, were separated now.

Clark lived on — a long, happy, and useful life. He was now deprived of his old comrade, it is true. But he had his devoted family. And he served first as commander of the militia; then for a time both as Superintendent of Indian Affairs in the West, and as Governor of Missouri. Immediately after Lewis's death, Clark felt it his duty to supervise the arrangements for the publication of their famous Journals, and to collaborate with Nicholas Biddle in the actual editing of these important papers.

He saw a little active service along the Mississippi in the War of 1812 and helped negotiate a peace with the Indians, when it was over. As Superintendent of Indian Affairs, he tried to keep the tribes peaceful, meanwhile forcing white squatters to refrain from trespassing on the tribal lands. He recovered stolen horses and kidnaped children, punished robbery and murder whether by whites or Indians, and tried to keep whiskey

from his redskinned friends. To the Indians he
became the "Red Head Chief," and he built up a
famous museum of Indian curiosities. Once the
Nez Percés, remembering the visit of Lewis and
Clark, sent a delegation to him in St. Louis, asking for a missionary. (In 1839, just after Clark's
death, the famous Father de Smet went out to
shepherd Indians, and, in the meantime, Protes-
tant missionaries had begun to work among the
Nez Percés and the tribes in Oregon.)

His beloved Julia died in 1820, after bearing
him five children, three of whom survived. It

was then that he married Harriet, who had been the other little girl with Julia on that balky horse on the Virginia road so many years ago. By Harriet he had two additional children.

After Harriet's death in 1831, Clark continued his Indian work, taking pride in the military career of his son, Meriwether Lewis Clark, who saw service in the Black Hawk War and (long after his father's death) as an officer in the Confederate Army. William Clark died in his son's home on September 1, 1838.

He died, that is, so far as such men can ever die.

One by one the members of the great expedition had dropped away — Lewis first of all, that mysterious night on the Tennessee frontier; Sacagawea a few years after; other explorers slain in further Indian adventures; still others in diverse ways, one by one.

Both officers had tried to aid their men in their readjustment to civilian American life when the expedition ended. Clark always tried to keep track of his old friends to know where and how they fared. He loved to recall the great adventure; and so did many of his men. All of their lives these explorers seem to have loved their old commander — combining in their affection the bond of soldiers and adventurers — a bond that those who have never served will never wholly comprehend.

It would be pleasant to imagine the two captains reassembling their gallant band on the shore of another and a greater river, after the even more mysterious expedition we all must take into a totally unknown country. Perhaps "all the trumpets sounded" for these pilgrims as the "sounden horn" once called them to their Christmas revels.

Many more stars now grace their country's flag. Ten of those stars symbolize states along the dangerous westward route over which they struggled, facing endless risk and misery. And even the latest two stars might never have been added to Old Glory's blue field, had not Lewis and Clark carried their flag overland to the great Pacific Ocean.

Other Books to Read

ORIGINAL JOURNALS OF THE LEWIS AND CLARK
EXPEDITION, edited by Reuben Gold Thwaites
(New York, 1904–5)
This edition contains seven volumes of text
and a volume of maps.

THE JOURNALS OF LEWIS AND CLARK, edited by
Bernard DeVoto (Boston, 1953)
A more convenient, and excellent, one-
volume edition of the most interesting parts
of the Journals.

LEWIS AND CLARK, PARTNERS IN DISCOVERY by
John Bakeless (New York, 1947)
This is the standard biography of Lewis and
Clark.

TWO CAPTAINS WEST by Albert and Jane Salisbury
(Seattle, 1950)
This book contains a fine collection of pic-
tures of the Lewis and Clark trail.

TALE OF VALOR by Vardis Fisher (New York,
1958)
A good novel based on the expedition.

INDEX

JOHN BAKELESS

Historian, editor, teacher and veteran of both World Wars, Colonel Bakeless always combined action with his intellectual pursuits.

He held three University degrees—an A.B. from Williams, and an M.A. and Ph.D. from Harvard—and was always interested in journalism. He was Literary Editor, Managing Editor, and Editor of *Living Age*, Literary Editor of the *Literary Digest*, Managing Editor of *Forum*, Literary Adviser of *The Independent*. He lectured on journalism and English at such institutions as New York University and Harvard, and was a published author from 1921.

In World War II, Bakeless was a general staff officer in Military Intelligence, War Department G-2. He saw service behind the German lines in Greece and with the Russians in Bulgaria, besides being assistant military attaché to Turkey. In Bulgaria he was Chief of the Military Section of the American Delegation of the Allied Control Commission. He had thirty-five years of army service, active and reserve.

Colonel Bakeless was born in 1894 in Carlisle, Pennsylvania. In his later years, he lived in Connecticut. He died in 1978.